Nia, Queen of the

The maiden voyage of *Nia Ben Aur*, named in memory of the beloved wife of her captain, is a poignant and emotional trip for Nia's family. For her elder child, Rhian, the trip is a time of transition, taking her from girl to woman, discovering love, betrayal, her own strength of character and, above all, a deeper understanding of her family and the ties that bind them to each other and the oceans.

Based on the authors' family history, *Nia, Queen of the Oceans* gives an important and fascinating insight into the lives of those from Porthmadoc, who relied on the trade routes for their living and of their families who sailed with them or waited, in hope, for their safe return.

N.S.E. (Nesta) Gwynne

was born in Cardiff in 1926. Her parents had moved from Porthmadog on their marriage, her father having left the Merchant Navy to work ashore. Her mother died in childbirth, a premature labour induced by a bomb falling on their home, leaving her husband to raise their three daughters. Nesta showed great academic ability, and following her mothers death, threw herself into her work. She was accepted at Cardiff University, aged 16, and studied Welsh and French. The war extended her studies and she graduated with honours, following a year in with a family in Brittany, in 1948. Nesta came to Durham City in 1949, to take up a post as librarian with the County Council. She married David, a vet, in 1952, and has 4 children and 9 grandchildren. This is Nesta's first novel.

Nia
Queen of the Oceans

BY N.S.E. GWYNNE

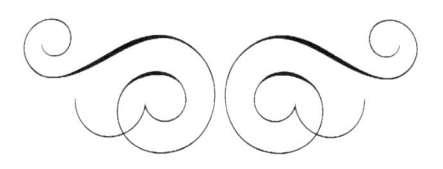

McFARLANE PRESS
DURHAM

First published 2005
© 2005 Nesta McFarlane
Published by McFarlane Press
Brecon View, Hillcrest, Claypath
Durham City

ISBN 0-9550444-0-5

Typeset by Koinonia, Bury
Printed in Great Britain by
The Doppler Press
Brentwood, Essex

*For my parents
Jenny and Tom*
whose family history and
love for each other and for
my sisters and myself,
inspired me
to tell their story

Acknowledgements

I should like to thank everyone who has helped me with the book. Dilys, Helen, Heather and Lisa for their energy and commitment in getting the dream out of my handwriting, into something that could be published. Alice and Lewis for their friendship and encouragement. Siân provided invaluable advice on modernising my Welsh translations Also the rest of my family, close and extended, who have supported me and believed in the book. Janet Allan, for her help and advice on the editing of the book. Steve Raw, for designing the cover. Lesley Kulig-Burston for the beautiful cover illustration. Peter, Jane, John and Paulette for assisting with the Canadian research, their hospitality and kindness. Owen for the help with distribution. Robert for designing the publicity information.

It has always been my intention to use sales of the book to support the Jubilee Sailing Trust , who do such splendid work and my grateful thanks are extended to Peter Davies, Trustee, for enabling me to do this. Capt. John Fisher's kindness in reviewing the nautical terms and the endorsement of the book by Tom Stewart, Chairman of the Trust, are greatly appreciated.

Lastly, to David, my husband, for pushing me to fulfil my dreams, despite the threat that my ever growing research files and books, would drive him out of hearth and home!

Routes of Nia & Olwen

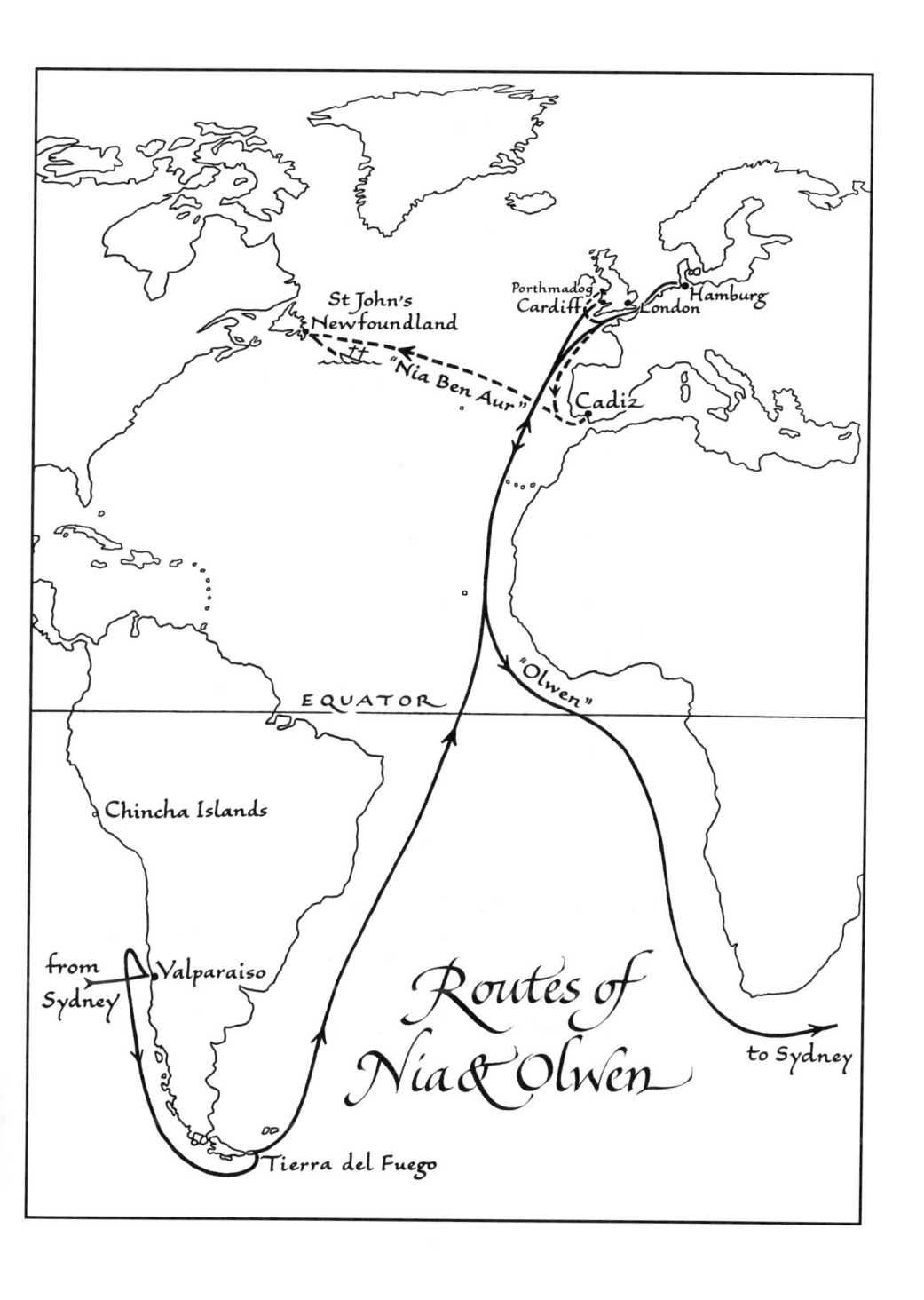

Characters

CREW OF THE OLWEN IN 1906

Captain	Rhys Morris
Mate	Brynley Hewitson
2nd Mate	Jack Beynon
Cook/Handyman	Bob Roberts (Uncle Choccy Bob)
Seamen:	Ifor
	Davy

CREW OF THE OLWEN IN 1913

Captain	Rhys Morris
Mate	Jack Beynon
2nd Mate	Ifor
Cook/Handyman	Bob Roberts (Uncle Choccy Bob)
Seamen:	Davy
	Peredur

CREW OF THE NIA BEN AUR

Captain & Owner	Rhys Morris, later Capt Mika Carlsen – known as Finn
Mate	Llew Bulkeley
2nd Mate	Ifor
Cook/Handyman	Bob Roberts (Uncle Choccy Bob)
Seamen:	Davy
	Peredur
	Guto

The Elkan Family (in Hamburg)

Grandparents:
Rosa Elkan , known as either Nanna or Oma
(Welsh and German)
Walter Elkan (Senior), known as Opa

Parents:
Walter Elkan (Junior)
Lisa Elkan (died in 1904 in childbirth)

Children:
Anja, Bernice, Henk, Vincent,

The Morris Family

Grandparents:
Lewis Morris also known as Taid
Sarah Morris also known as Nain

Parents:
Captain Rhys Morris also known as Tada
Nia Morris nee De Winton also known as Mam

2nd Wife: Marrion

Children with Nia:
Rhian, Owen

Children with Marrion:
Twins Sarah and Rosa

Step Daughter:
Cathy, daughter of Marrion

Chapter One

Tada's new ship was being launched. We had watched her being built, Nain [*granny*] and me, all through the winter months. She was so beamy amidships, and yet so elegant on the water, even without her masts, that they had to launch her sideways into the harbour, something that had only once been attempted in Porthmadog before, so Nain had been on her knees every night for a week or more, – I could hear her, from my bed up in the attic, chanting her prayers.

Owen was being a little monster! He'd been entranced for months – years! – with the whole business. He spent all his time at the Cei [*the quay*], after school, and now, as we walked to the great moment, dressed in our best, of course, he pranced along backwards, taunting me. "You haven't seen her finished – I have!"

"Rubbish", I said, as dignified, as a grown-up sister should be.

"You don't know," he chanted, just wait till you see her"

Tada had arrived home two days before. They'd held up the launch, knowing he was due. This was his first ship all of his own. Uncle Morris Chandler's, and William Lloyd, across the road from us, each had a share in his old ship, the *Olwen*, but Uncle Morris had died, and William Lloyd's son was off to College, in London, so Tada [*Dad*] managed on his own. Lots of the Mutual Club members were getting very worried, because of the steamships that were being built, instead of the sailing ships, which had always sailed out of Porthmadog, but Tada still felt proud of the old sailing ships, especially the wooden hulled ships. Queens of the ocean he called them. Of course, some of the new sailing ships over the last years had hulls of steel, but Tada had so often been glad that his timbers would stay afloat, that he had a horror of steel coffins! People will always find room for sailing ships, they are so beautiful, so graceful, and I felt so proud as we went down past the Town Hall to the water's edge.

All our friends were there, everyone smiling and laughing, and Nain's eyes were lit up like the bonfire on Guy Fawkes night.

The Boy Scouts and the Cubs were there, and Owen joined them, sitting in the front row, right in front of the flag. The town band was there too, and Rhiannon, my best friend, and when she started singing

"Ar Hyd y Nos" [*All through the night*], I couldn't help myself: I just joined in. Rhiannon and I often sing duets together, and I soared into the descant, which she had composed for me. When we finished, I was quite taken aback. Eirian Terfel, the band leader bowed to Rhiannon; the crowd clapped wildly. Then he turned and bowed to me, and they all clapped again. I was blushing, but I was thrilled to the marrow too. Then Tada stepped up, and at last we knew the great secret: he named his ship *Nia Ben Aur* [*Nia with the golden hair*], after my mother – our mother, Owen's and mine. I heard such a sigh, and turned. I thought Nain, my granny was going to faint, she was so pale, but her eyes filled up with tears. Then Tada bent down, and gently lifted the ensign away at the bows.

I looked ... I looked ... I couldn't look away. All the years I had thought I couldn't remember her ... and here she was. I could see her, as beautiful as ever ... Her eyes full of excitement and wonder, straining forward to see what lay ahead ... the wind stirring her long golden hair. Her voice said to me, "Wel di'r dolffins, cariad (Look at the dolphins, sweetheart)?" and suddenly my breath wouldn't come. I felt the quay rise to meet me, and then Nain's arms were tight around me. She said not a word, and I looked. She was gazing at me. "Never forget", she said, "You two are all he has left of her."

Owen's hand wriggled into mine, the way he used to do, when he was little. He had abandoned the Scouts. "I told you!" he said, his imp's face bursting with mischief. "I heard them say that the figurehead was coming up on the train first thing this morning, and Griff and I sneaked out to watch them fit it, at Mr. Williams' yard.

"Rhian" he said in wonder, "was she really like that, our Mam, was she really beautiful like that?" "Just like that, Owen," I said. "Beautiful as that ... and fun, and loving, and gentle, and ... ". I wanted to say more, but I was afraid he wouldn't understand ... You don't, do you, at eight years old? And then they were breaking the bottle of Madeira wine, that Tada had brought back from one of his long voyages and I felt Nain still as a statue beside me as she willed everything to go well for Tada, and all who would sail in his ship.

And then *Nia Ben Aur* plunged proudly and elegantly into the water. The wave crests sparkled like a fountain of shooting stars, and as she settled lightly into the flow of the tide, the band played "Yn y dyfroedd mawr, a'r tonnau ... (in the heaving waters, full of waves ...)" and suddenly her voice was in my head, singing. Mam always sang it when the watch changed, and I went to my bed, as the stars came out. She would lie beside me, on their bed – hers and Tada's – in the Captain's cabin, and by the time she whispered the last words, I was in wonderland, out there with the stars and the moon.

Afterwards, we all went to the Oakleys, Tada's friends, for a celebration tea, there on the quayside. It was set out like a picnic, in their garden, which overlooks Ballast Island. The flowers of the orchids, from Hawaii, and of the gardenias from the Pacific Islands, which had been carried by generations of seamen from this little country, made memories flicker once again in the back of my mind, but I found it easier to concentrate on the bara brith (fruit loaf), and the delicious cakes set out for us.

Tada came and joined us, and Uncle Bob – Uncle Choccy Bob we called him, because he always brought us chocolate bars – and the men who had sailed with Tada over the years came to share Tada's joy in his ship.

Tada came over. He lifted me up and swung me round, just as he did when I was Owen's age. "What do you think, cariad? Isn't she a ship to be proud of!" I burst in "I remember her ... How did you get the carving so real, so beautiful so ... " He looked at me, his eyes full of love and wonder. "When you want to see her, just look in the mirror, Rhian fach", and he smiled at me. "Except for your hair, of course. The fiery chestnut mane is mine!"

Owen came tearing up. "Isn't she splendid Tada. I saw her this morning, when she came on the train. Finn carved her ... Pity he couldn't bring her himself ... he's got a ship sailing from Cardiff today." Tada looked down at us "You remember Finn then?" "Of course," said Owen, "He was mate on the *Olwen* with you."

Tada looked at me "And you, Rhian, do you remember Finn?" Surprised, I said, "Yes, of course. Well, I don't know him very well. He stays with Mrs. Morgan at the shop, when he's ashore doesn't he? I didn't know he did carvings, though ... Someone at school said he'd gone on the expedition to the Antarctic" "Yes," said Tada, "but before that, do you remember ... " and then Captain Oakley interrupted. The photographer from the 'Cambrian News' was waiting to take our pictures, and when all the excitement was over we went home to Nain's house in Chapel Street.

Chapter Two

Having to go back to school was excruciating at first, but I loved school, especially poetry, Welsh and English literature, – and German, and French, – and history, and geography.

My special friends were Jenny Hughes, the harbour master's daughter, and Rhiannon Owen, whose dad was the farrier. We were all in the same class, but Rhiannon was two years older than us. She lived in Penmorfa, a good way out of Porthmadog, so she wasn't able to come to school in the winter, until she was six years old.

Rhiannon and I didn't get on at all well, when I first came to live with Nain. The other girls started to call her Non, so that Rhiannon and Rhian didn't get muddled. "It makes us sound like Siamese twins in the circus" she said. "Besides, I'm Rhiannon; I'm older, and I was here first. You should call *her* 'Not-Non!'". I giggled so much over this that we made friends through our laughter. In the springtime Rhiannon showed me where the black rabbits burrowed in the banks at Penmorfa, and I grew to love watching them, in the early morning.

It was through Rhiannon that I learned that I could sing, and write poetry, and when I won my first bardic chair at our school Eisteddfod, under my nom-de-plume, 'Not-Non', we both knew that we were friends for life! We had exams to sit at the end of the summer term, for our school certificate, and matriculation. Rhiannon would be leaving school, but Jenny and I were going to stay on for another year or possibly two, and go on to college at Bangor.

At sundown, I loved to go down to the harbour; my excuse was to bring Owen home. I would linger there with Jenny, to watch *Nia Ben Aur* being fitted out at William Groom's yard. We usually chatted with the young men as they came away from work. Jenny was very fond of Peredur Williams, whose young brother Griff was Owen's best friend at school. One evening a male voice choir came up from Cyfarthfa in South Wales. We had a wonderful night of singing, with Eirian Terfel and the town band accompanying them. As the moon came up we all joined in. Suddenly Eirian pointed his baton at our groups of school friends. The visitors fell silent: Eirian led the band into the first notes, and then Rhiannon's voice soared into the night sky; even the stars and the moon seemed to shine brighter in delight as she sang. She stretched out her hand to me, and without my usual agonies of shyness, I sang with her "Holl amranatau'r sêr ddywedent, ar hyd y nôs ... Dyma'r ffordd i fro gogoniant ... [*All the constellations of stars sing, right through the night, this is the path to the glory of heaven, all through the night*]" and truly it seemed that this music of the stars was the way to heaven.

We had a wonderful celebration. At its end, Rhiannon had promised that she would sing her heart out – but taking care of her throat and lungs, she joked, – while taking singing lessons from a professional teacher until her parents felt she was ready to go to Cardiff, or even London. And the very next day, word came that the wife of Mr. Casson, a very famous actress, had heard the music, and would sponsor Rhiannon in her career.

Three weeks later we had finished our exams, and school was over for this year. Tada had succeeded in selling *Olwen* and was on his way back to us from Appledore where he had delivered her to her new owners. *Olwen* had many happy memories for him, but she was no longer viable for the new trade in salt and fish and timber, which was all that was left to the wooden sailing vessels. Iron hulls, driven by steam engines had taken over the world of ocean trade. It was only in the tiny harbours of Newfoundland that the wooden ships could compete. The Panama Canal would spare the need for the perilous trips round the Horn, which had claimed so many seamen's lives: As Tada said, the picture was not entirely black.

We went to the Eisteddfod Genedlaethol for Rhiannon to enter the young musicians singing competition. It was the first time I had been to the Eisteddfod. Grandma De Winton thought it "Unduly Welsh", as I remember. Everyone thought Rhiannon would be a great opera singer one day: she came second in her class, which was the stuff of fables for someone so young and inexperienced. One of three sons of a local farmer came second in the poetry competition for the chair, too. It was so exciting. He was sitting beside us in the pavilion when they said how wonderful his poem was, and how difficult it was to choose a winner. His nom-de-plume was Hedd Wyn, and Rhiannon said, "Perhaps we'll both be first in next year's competitions". He smiled at her, and said, "Shall we work on that together when we get back home? I could come down to Penmorfa from Trawsfynydd at the weekend … " Jenny and I looked at one another, and Jenny's eyebrows arched right up to her curly fringe! Little did we know then that they would fall in love, and how sad would be his story. As things were, we set off again for home; we went as we had come; on the train, but Rhiannon and her mother rode home with Elsyn, her new Romeo, in his trap.

Chapter Three

If going back to school was bad for me, it was much worse for Owen. "Dull as ditchwater after all the excitement!" he said to me. At least I had my examinations to keep me busy. I was hoping to do well enough to train to be a schoolteacher, after I'd done my Highers.

Owen was down at David Williams' Yard at the quay as soon as school finished every single day. I kept up with how the rigging was going, too, because as soon as supper was ready every evening Nain sent me down to fetch him home.

Tada had promised to take us over to Canada as soon as the ship was rigged and registered and ready to sail – the three 'R's' he called it! We were going over to meet his new wife. I'd been quite happy about her before. Tada had been a lonely person for as long as I can remember.

But now it was different. It seemed strange to be remembering my Mam, just when Tada was moving on to take a new wife. Somehow I was glad that someone would remember her. The more the pictures of her re-appeared in my head, the more I knew that Grandma De Winton, her mother, my grandma, remembered a different Nia – perhaps the girl she was before she and Tada met: before she became a woman, and my Mam. I tried to say so, feeling there was something going mad in my head, but Nain knew straight away what I meant.

While Tada was away, delivering *Olwen* to her new owners in Appledore, John Morris, the sailmakers, had quoted a price for over a hundred and twenty pounds for the new sails. Nain contacted Tada, and said that several friends had offered to put up money, in exchange for a share in the ownership, but Tada was like granite! He had always longed to have his very own ship, and he was not going to give up now.

That night Nain came up to my bedside in the attic. She knelt on the floor and wrapped her arms round me. "Listen, Rhian fach" she said. "This is just between two ladies who love your Tada … " I cut in sharply: "Two ladies … ?" I asked, uncertainly. "You and me, cariad," she smiled "Who were you thinking of?" "You, of course, Nain … and my Mam … but she's dead … Marrion, over in Canada … but surely if she had money to spare she would have given it already … Grandma De

Winton? ... Oh no, not her ... " All the possibilities had flashed through my mind ... "Me, Nain? I haven't got any money, more's the pity. I wish I could help ... "

' Before you sailed the last time Nia, your mammy, asked me to look after her special ring. She wanted you to have it, if anything happened to her. I've said nothing till now, but ... "

"Mam's ring?", I said. "Mam's ring ... ?" I shut my eyes, not meaning to, they just shut themselves. "With the green stone ... ?" Nain looked at me, love in her eyes, "She's coming back into your life, isn't she, my lovely. Don't turn her away ... Love her now as you did then ... and as she loved you then, and loves you still." "Nain," I said, "don't be daft! How can you know what she feels now!"

"Rhian," said Nain "Do I love you?"

"Oh, Nain", "that's not fair, that's not what I meant."

Nain said again, "Do I love you?" "Yes, I know you do, Nain annwyl," I said, because she looked so stern.

"Do you love me?" she said. "Nain" I whispered, aghast. "You cannot ask such a thing ... I can not believe that you could doubt that ... "

"Exactly," she nodded "I know, in just that same way, that Nia loves you ... that nothing will come to you, ever, from Nia, your Mam, but love! ... To you and to Owen. Never forget that ... never doubt it".

"Oh, Nain, do you think if we had come to you when she died, that I wouldn't have forgotten ... "

Nain stopped me "You never have forgotten her ... never, never ... the memories are just tucked away in your head, until you can face the sadness of remembering them: till you can face remembering the happiness of being with her".

If anyone but Nain had said it I would have wanted to die, but Nain loved her, and loved me, and Tada, and Owen ...

And suddenly Mam's face was there, in my head, smiling not at me, but with me.

"Mam ... Nain ... I know that's what she ... ". I don't think I even said it out loud, but Nain knew ... "How much will we get from the ring? Will it be enough?" "Yes", said Nain "It is Welsh gold, from Dolau Cothi, and the emerald is a fine one. I think she would have liked you to have it when you find who you love and marry, but some things are just as important."

And so, Tada found that Nain had enough money put by, to buy the sails for *Nia Ben Aur*. We smiled secretly at one another …

"My shares in the ship will be unwritten," she winked at me

"And they will be Rhian's when she marries. You are our witness, Owen. So if you hope to own your own ship one day, keep her sweet on you!"

I couldn't help wondering whether Owen would have to be just a ship's captain, for one of the big ship companies, when he grew up.

Chapter Four

On the following Monday, Tada arrived home; he had travelled straight to Liverpool by train, to complete all arrangements for registration of *Nia Ben Aur* with Lloyds. She was listed as A1, as Tada's ships had always been, and he had hitched a lift from his friend Tommy Roberts, the captain of the "Rebecca", the little steamship that sailed into Port every Monday, with goods for sale. Down at the wharf, next morning, they were already sliding the bundles of slates, ten in each bundle, down the wide planks into the hold of *Nia Ben Aur*, for shipment to Hamburg. Tada always liked to cushion the bundles with bracken, to stop the slates moving in a storm. Such a solid, heavy cargo could sink a ship in no time at all, if it shifted in the hold, but Porthmadog seamen had been taking slates to Hamburg ever since the great fire of 1842, over seventy years by now, and they had learned the hard way, many of them, to stow this cargo as safely as anyone could. Tada was eager to get away. Nain, too, said so many unpleasant things were happening at present and that she would be very relieved when we got back again! For the last weeks, she had been feeding us up with potatoes mashed up with llaeth enwyn, or buttermilk, and with apples and oranges, home made lemonade, runner beans, peas, lettuce, cabbage, raspberries and strawberries all straight from the allotment. As we got ready to head off to the quayside she produced a veritable hatchery of fresh eggs carefully packed in a basket, which she handed to Tada to carry, and a wrapped parcel, which later I found, contained homemade cyflaith – treacle toffee – a favourite of both Owen and me. She walked steadily down to Pen Cei [*the quay's end*] with us, then as we embarked, she made her way slowly up Grisia' Mawr [*the Big Steps*], where she turned at the top, and waved, throwing us a kiss as she did so. I knew where we would see her again. She would be waving to us as we sailed on the tide, from Craig y Don [*the headland*]. Once we were over the bar, the pilot cast us loose, and we were on our way.

The weather was anything but promising. My little brother surprises me sometimes. He insists he is *Owen*, not to be called by his "baby" name of Oggie ever again. He cast a last look back at Porthmadog, and said rather sadly, "Nain will be alright on her own, won't she Tada?" When Tada reassured him, he raced off to join the men, as they set the sails.

As soon as Nain's little figure had faded out of sight, and I had given her a last frantic wave, we moved to the bow of the ship, to look ahead, out to sea, out to the future. For a while, though, it seemed that all I could see was the past! The seagulls didn't help; they were crying like tiny drowning kittens, rather than birds who could take wing whenever they fancied.

I had been left behind so many times in my sixteen years ... No, I thought, I'm not being left ... I'm the one sailing off. Somehow it felt just as lonely, leaving the happiest home I could remember. I shut the thoughts out, for fear of bringing about my nightmare, that Nain would not be there to meet us, when we came home again.

The wind was gusting in the sails, and the sea was choppy, as if to test *Nia Ben Aur*, on her maiden voyage. Even Owen began to weary of the seesaw motion by teatime, when we struggled on past St Tudwal's roads.

Suddenly, just as we had cleared Pen Cilan, the wind swung round, and blew steadily from the north, filling our sails, so that we were bowling along. *Nia Ben Aur* seemed to glide over the waves – it felt like Atalanta's race! Neither Owen nor I could bear to go below: it was so exciting, so much to see.

I stood beside this wonderful carving of Nia, and found my hands reaching out to stroke the oaken curve of her head and breast. I wondered why Grandma De Winton, who after all was her mother, had remembered only the withdrawn cool correct young lady in the portrait in her drawing room, and not this free loving spirit who was Nia, my mother. I had been, I realised now, so frightened and bereft by her death that I had forgotten – well almost – because I had remembered promising her that I would care for her baby until Tada came ashore.

I looked over to Owen. I had managed that for her, anyway. I had managed to keep the balance between Owen, the natural rebel, and Grandma De Winton, to whom it mattered so much to "belong". It wasn't until three years ago, when Auntie Nan, Mam's younger sister, married her newly created baronet, and produced a son to inherit, and Grandma decided to move to Cheshire, to be near them, that she sent

Owen and me back to live with Nain and Tada. That had changed my obstreperous little brother totally, and for the better.

His face, now, as he stood beside Tada was alight. He was watching the shoreline ahead, and the horizon. I had always thought he must inherit his wild love of the sea, and space, and adventure from Tada, but as I stood beside Mam's figurehead, I saw it was quite as much from her.

"You can see why the sun sets in the west, can't you, Rhian" he called to me. "That's the place to go!"

"Tir N'an Og", – the Land of Eternal Youth", I agreed, as we sailed into the gold and flaming fires of the western sky. The wind had started to sing a shade fiercer as we turned south, and the sails, which Tada had set in hope, rather than in expectation, seemed to swell and sing like a choir of angel voices. We were heavy laden with the slates, but our graceful little ship seemed to glide along. The steam ship "Sylvia", bound for Cadiz, which had motored past us an hour ago, when we were struggling against the heavy wind, and the head seas, was soon left ploughing along like an old carthorse, while *Nia Ben Aur* danced over the waves like an Arab pony.

Uncle Choccy Bob brought up a wonderful supper of "tatws-cig-yn-popty" [*lamb and potatoes cooked in the oven*], served still in the meat tin in which the potatoes, onions, and the Welsh lamb had been roasted. We all sat there, on deck, in the sun's glow, to eat, helping ourselves with spoons and our fingers, and dipping our bread in the gravy.

Tada was at the wheel himself; not usual I gathered for the master; he wanted to sail his new ship out to the safety of the open seas himself, this first voyage. "Let's hope she's as happy a ship as *Olwen* was, for your Dad's sake, said Uncle Bob, and then he poured all six of us a glass of Madeira wine: the first I'd tasted – well, to remember anyway! "The Captain will enjoy his when the watch is done" he said.

So we sailed on into the great world. As it grew dark, neither Owen nor I could bear to go below. The stars seemed to be lighting a path to the moon, so we brought our blankets out, and curled up, in the bow of the ship. Tada was still on deck with us, but his new second in command was on watch. His name is Llew Bulkeley. He comes from a family of ship-agents from Anglesey, and his mother and Grandma De

Winton were friends from long ago.

"How will we get to Hamburg from here, Tada?" I heard Owen ask. "Well" said Tada, "There are two ways: we could have turned north when we passed Pen Cilan, and sailed up past Caer Gybi [*Holyhead*], and the Isle of Man, and right among the Scottish islands – the Hebrides, the Orcades, and then headed South and East, across the Great Fisher Bank, to the mouth of the Elbe. We call that going North about. But this time we are going south, down the coast of Wales, round the toe of Cornwall, through the English Channel, and from there North and East, past Dogger Bank in the North Sea, to the River Elbe, again. And then we'll sail up the river, past Hamburg docks, to our sailing ship harbour, which is called Harburg".

Nain had taught me to know the stars, as part of her navigation course. Grandma De Winton liked to look down her nose at Nain Morris; "a simple Welsh countrywife" was a description I'd heard from her, but in truth, Nain had taught navigation to many of the young men from Porthmadog, Borth-y-Gest, Nefyn, most of Lleyn, in fact. Those who hoped to become sea captains had come to her father's School of Navigation, where she helped him in the instruction. When he died, Nain had carried on. The mariners who went on to the newer merchant navy Training Schools from Nain's school in our front room always did well in navigation.

This last year, Owen had sat and listened, and asked questions. Now, with this wonderful clear vault of the night sky above us – no smoke, no clouds – I helped him name all the stars, as Nain had taught us.

"Where is the Southern Cross then, Rhian?" he said.

"You have to cross the equator to see some of the stars", I answered, "so you won't see the Southern Cross this voyage." I couldn't help smiling: not much passes by my little brother's cocked ears.

I had my back against the cabin, and Owen was curled up beside me. We sang all Nain's old songs, and when I started on "Huna, forwr llong, hun ar yr eigion ... [*sleep, my sailor, sleep on the waves*]". I felt his head droop on my shoulder.

"See, Mam", I whispered, looking at her figure, outlined against the night sky, "I promised: and I think he's great, don't you, Mammy?"

Behind me Tada's hand caressed my head. I hadn't heard him come up – don't know how long he'd been listening to us. His eyes were full of love as he looked down at us. He didn't say anything; just went forward and stood beside her figure head, and I heard him sing; it was a song I'd never heard before: It didn't even sound Welsh ... I caught a few of the words ... "wert thou in the cauld blast ... I'd shelter thee, I'd shelter thee ... to share it a' ... to share it a' ... ", and then as the wind whipped his voice to me "Sae black and bare, sae black and bare, the desert were a paradise, if thou wert there, if thou wert there ... "

As his voice drifted away, Tada looked at me

"Nia must be the proudest Mother in the whole of heaven, proud of you both, cariad" he said, "you and Owen."

We carried Owen below, and Tada put him onto the bunk he'd insisted on having, in the fo'csle with the young men of the crew.

Tada and I came on deck again. We would soon be heading into the Atlantic swell, off Saint David's head, and even though Llew Bulkeley was on his watch, Tada wanted to see how his new ship faced the rougher seas. There was so much to see and to feel: I couldn't bear to miss anything, so we sailed through this wonderful night, just the three of us.

Chapter Five

We were cracking along at nine knots by the time I woke, got dressed and up on deck. Davy was on watch, with Peredur to help him.

"This watch, in the morning, from four o'clock is my favourite time" said Peredur, as I came on deck.

"I like it because you get to see the sun come, and there's often lots of things to do. You get to think about the day's sailing, and where we'll be by tonight." He smiled shyly. "When we're close to the land like this, there's lots of birds to watch, and dolphins sometimes, and always seals."

Peredur is such a quiet person, but he's not dull to be with. He's seventeen, two years older than me, and was in the class above me, until he left to go to sea, but he seems more grown-up than most of his old school friends.

The boys at our school are lucky: they don't have to wear uniform like us, just a school badge on their caps. We have to wear long navy blue serge skirts, and white blouses, and thick woolly stockings that make my legs itch like mad.

"Did you always want to be a sailor, Peredur?" I asked, because his father's not a seaman, he keeps the Chemist's shop, in the High Street.

"No Rhian, I didn't, and I still don't want to, really" he answered.

"Do you know what I'd like. I'd like to a be a flier."

"In an air-plane?" I said in amazement.

"Yes", he came back at me. "'member at the Show, on the Traeth last year, when that German chap flew his plane – Gustav Harmel his name was. I'd love to have a plane like that. I thought if I work on the ships till I'm a bit older, and can get a few pounds saved, I can join some Air Cadets, or Flying Cadets, or something, and learn to fly."

"That's a great idea" I said. I hadn't ever thought of Peredur as someone who would want to try something so new, and so exciting. I suppose it's because he's quiet: he never lets you know what he's dreaming about.

Davy came over then, and we could see the coastline. It was nearly breakfast time, but we were off St. David's Head, and the scenery in the morning sunlight was magical. I knew I ought to go below, and help Uncle Bob, but I couldn't make myself leave. A boat passed us. It had families aboard who waved, and we waved back. I think it must be a ferryboat that goes over to Ireland. Just to the south, the Bird Islands came into view, Skomer, and Skokholm. Davy and Peredur knew all the birds: besides the sea-gulls, there were gannets, and puffins, and oystercatchers and shearwaters, which I had never seen before, and then we saw lots of seals on the rocky shore, and dolphins swimming in the water around us. There was a little island, too, and as we sailed past we heard thousands of gannets, screeching like banshees.

By the time Davy had helped us to name all the lighthouses we could smell Uncle Bob's breakfast cooking in the galley. I went down for mine, and found Tada there already halfway through his meal, together with Guto, who was to take the next watch with him, at eight bells. Owen was there too. He was like Guto's shadow.

"Did you sleep well in the berth in the foc'sle?" I asked Owen.

"Like those bats in the barn" he replied. "Even Guto's snoring didn't keep me awake."

Guto nudged him. "Watch it, Owen Morris" he retorted. "I'll tell your big sister what you dreamed about!" They both went off into fits of the giggles.

"Boys!", I thought, but kept the words to myself. It's strange to see my little brother growing up, being with the older lads.

The day seemed to disappear. There were so many things to see, to do, and to learn. We sailed across the mouth of the Bristol Channel, all sails set, the abaft-the-beam wind making *Nia Ben Aur* dance through the waves. At one point the deck was awash, as we cut through the waters and by first dog-watch on the second day out of port, we were off the coast of Cornwall.

The cliffs at Pendeen, and even more so at Botallack Head, reminded me of Blaenau Ffestiniog and Bethesda. The mine shafts running right down to the shore.

The breeze which was so kind to us, bowling us along, smacked wildly when it hit the cliffs, so that I felt sorry for the tin miners down there.

"I bet it's like being buried in a coffin, and when the wind blows like this, I bet it sounds as if you'll never get out alive!", I said to Llew Bulkeley, who was on deck beside me.

"The tin's very valuable, though", he answered, "and I should think these men are glad to have work, to keep their stomachs full", he observed.

Personally, as we passed Botallack, I thought the red and yellow bricks of the engine house looked unsuitably cheerful.

We sailed on south, past Cape Cornwall, to round Land's End, and then on the horizon we could glimpse the Islands of Scilly, while on our lee-side, we left the Longships Lighthouse.

Once again our luck held. The wind changed soon after we had gybed to shape a course up the English Channel, and once more we were romping along at top speed.

I had helped Uncle Bob to prepare the supper before coming on deck, and now I sat down with the men to eat mine, as we came up to the second dog watch, at six o'clock.

It was lamb and cacen 'nionod – onion cake – a great favourite of Owen's, and to follow we had the last of Nain's bara brith, a lovely fruit loaf, sliced and buttered with tasty Welsh salty butter. We all finished off with a large mug of tea.

"Great", and "Champion", were the comments of Owen and Guto as they tucked in.

Llew Bulkeley had done the first dog watch, with Peredur, so we had to leave enough for them.

Tada sat with Uncle Bob, next to the stove, and when they lit up their pipes at the end, and strolled away up on deck, Ifor said

"Mind now, you two, you won't always get food like this when you're on board ship, will they, Davy!"

"Good God, no," said Davy, "and mind, when the food really runs out, which of them would make the best pot of lobscouse, d'you think, Ifor?"

"I think perhaps Owen bach," replied Ifor. "He's not so stringy as Guto."

"Yes, but", said Davy "there's more of Guto, if we were really hungry ... "

"We wouldn't get to choose, any rate" commented Ifor. "Old Bob the Shambles there would cut off the tastiest parts with his carving knife and throw the rest in the stew pot. He'd decide which one went in first, not you or me!"

The two boys had been silenced at first, but suddenly they realised they were having their legs pulled, and with a howl they threw themselves at their tormentors – both landing on Davy who was not as quick to disappear up the steps as Ifor.

He escaped unchallenged, but I thought he'd pay for the teasing later on, knowing my little brother. Somehow it made me realise why Owen wanted to be with the crew. I envied him as I watched Ifor and Davy, the experienced seamen, teaching Guto and Owen the uses of the different knots, the importance of rigging the canvas to maximise safety and speed, explaining the winds and the tides. Peredur, too, who was often on the watch on deck, when the lads were off, showed them the flow of the currents, the lighthouses and lightships to be watched for, the "feel" of the steering, the set of the shrouds – all things you can't really learn half as well from books.

We finished our supper by the time Llew and Peredur came below, but I stayed to help Uncle Bob dish up.

Ifor and Davy, and Peredur have sailed before with Tada, but Llew is new, and not being a Porthmadog man, he is a little out of things. When he smiles at me he's like Douglas Fairbanks at the pictures! Ifor and Davy are what Nain would call "pobol y werin", and Grandma De Winton would call "rustic" – in spite of the fact that they are seamen, and each about to claim his Mate's Certificate! I imagine the top and bottom of it is that Llew is wealthier than the Porthmadog lads, and more used to "company": what Rhiannon would call the "Crachach" the Crust interpret that as you will! Funny, I can hear her voice in my head.

Anyway, I sat with the two of them, yarning away while they ate and Uncle Bob started the clearing up. They were talking about Patras, and Cadiz as well as Hamburg and Boston, and I marvelled at how much of the world someone as young as Peredur had seen, in the three years he had been at sea.

Llew was saying "Of course, it's bound to come. Steamships will put the sailing fleet into museums, and before too long, at that."

"For trade, perhaps," said Peredur, "but sailing ships are blown along by the free winds, while steamers have to have coal, which is expensive, and expendable. What happens when we run out of coal?"

"The engineers will come up with something else" was Llew's opinion. "Perhaps it'll be wind again, or sunshine."

"Or even water," chuckled Uncle Bob "there's plenty of water about when you're at sea!"

"I suppose if the worst came to the worst we could go back to manpower. Better get our Captain's Certificates before that happens, Peredur", said Llew. "I'd rather be the man cracking the whip than one of the banks of oarsmen".

I couldn't help laughing, and so did Peredur, but as soon as they had gone out, Uncle Bob frowned

"He'd enjoy it, too, that one. You watch out for him, Rhian fach. I can see he fancies the owner's daughter!"

I just smiled and shrugged my shoulders. I wondered how old Mam was, when she and Tada fell in love.

I went then to the Captain's cabin, sat on my bed, and wrote up my diary, keeping company with Tada who was writing up the ship's log.

When we had finished I brushed my hair, and went up on deck, where the moon was full. We all wandered on the deck, as we passed by the lights of the Isle of Wight. Davy got out his mouth organ, Uncle Bob unwrapped his squeezebox, and we all sat singing and just watching the world go by.

Llew came and sat beside me, and I found myself cuddling into the curve of his arm, as the hours passed in pleasure. I enjoyed feeling the warmth of his breath on my cheek. The boys were singing the old shanties: "Ranso was a school-boy" was Owen's favourite … "He ran away from school, boys, Ranso boys, Ranso" he sang with great glee, and when they came to "They … … … … … … … … … and keelhauled him … " he and Guto threw themselves cheekily at Ifor, threatening to do just that. Well, I said they'd catch up with him sometime!

At last midnight came. Llew took over the watch again, with Peredur. A day for a princess, if not yet a queen, I thought to myself, as Tada kissed me goodnight, and I watched the dark world pass slowly by.

Chapter Six

We finally arrived at the mouth of Elbe on Saturday, just in time to take the pilot aboard, to take us up the river to Hamburg, and from there the pilot's steam tug took us through the main port to the sailing ship quay at Hamburg.

Uncle Walter Elkan was on the quayside to welcome us. At the time when the Embankment was built by William Madocks, and the harbour at Porthmadog became the shipping port for Ffestiniog slates, there was a great fire in Hamburg, and from that time, about 1842, I think, our little schooners had listed Harburg as their regular first port of call, heavy laden with slates to re-roof the new buildings of Hamburg.

As a result, Porthmadog families and the shipping agents in Hamburg and their families have been friends for nearly seventy years, now.

Grandma Elkan had made Nain's wedding dress, way back in the 1870s, and Nain still had it, wrapped up and stored away in her treasure cupboard.

We all had quilted silk Sunday-best "tea-cosy" berets that she and her daughters had made for us.

As soon as the Excise officers, and other port authorities had welcomed us, the sun went down behind the grey-blue Welsh slate roofs of the city, and Uncle Walter insisted on taking us home for the night, Tada, Owen and me, that is, and Uncle Bob. Llew remained on board, in charge, with Ifor, Davy, Peredur and Guto.

Nanna Elkan came to meet us at the door, to welcome us with hugs and kisses. Her eyes fell on me, and her face lit up in a smile. "*Nia gwallt goch*!" [*Nia with the red hair*] she said, struggling with the Welsh sounds, and rather cleverly covering my likeness to Nia, my mother, and my inheritance of Tada's chestnuts locks. Then she smiled at me, with one of those smiles that you know is not just polite, but full of real love and friendship. I remembered Nanna Elkan so clearly. She and Nain were great friends – had been friends since they both got married in the same year, and had had to select different dates, so that Opa Elkan could be best man at Taid's wedding, and Taid, my grandfather, could return the compliment at Oma and Opa [*grandmother and grandfather*]

Elkan's wedding. Just about four years ago, when we moved to live with her in Porthmadog, Nain had brought Owen and me to Hamburg for a holiday, and we stayed with Nanna Elkan, so I remembered her, and the rest of the family quite well; I'm not sure how much of that holiday Owen remembers, but he very soon made friends with the grandsons, who were there.

The next few days were hectic unloading the slate and loading the new cargo and then on Saturday, how she knew, I can't even guess, but Nanna Elkan, said as it was Uncle Bob's birthday, we should all have a bonfire, and a picnic. Uncle Walter would arrange for two of his own men to stay aboard the ship, so that the rest of the crew could join us.

Uncle Walter sent two taxicabs down to the quay to take us up the hill to the old house, and when we got there the bonfire was well alight. "Rhian, look, isn't it wonderful", Owen's voice danced with delight, and he grasped my hand, and Guto's hand, and tore through the garden to the paved area where the table was laid with every treat that a crew of healthy hungry young men, about to set out on a long sea-voyage, could dream of.

I was taken by surprise, and almost measured my length in a most undignified heap, when a helping hand reached out and caught me, clasping me tight. As I turned to say thank you, I realised that the arms about me were too strong for Tada, or for Uncle Bob. I had to lean a little closer, to turn around to see who had come to my rescue. "Thank you … " I started to say, and as I turned I was held close in Llew Bulkeley's arms. My heart was leaping in my breast: I felt as if I was floating on a pathway of stars. We stood for what seemed then a lifetime, but later on I felt almost cheated by Owen's cry, "Come on, Rhian, Nanna Elkan's here waiting to know what you want!" "Thank you, Llew," I smiled tremulously. He smiled back "Buck, to my best friends" he said "ever since my favourite little visitor, many years ago, at my sister's birthday party, said "Llew … the Lion … will he bite me?"

And suddenly I remembered: just before we came back to live with Nain and Tada, going to my friend Helen's birthday party, and meeting her cousin – The Lion among them!

He seemed grown up then, to me, – the gap in our ages seemed to have narrowed! He must have been seventeen or eighteen then, and I would be nine years old, near enough, and that unhappy, withdrawn young madame, still …

He grinned at me. "I didn't fancy a bite then, but I might make you pay for the remark now"; and his eyes mocking me, he gently nibbled at my neck.

I couldn't help giggling, but I felt flattered too, and strangely roused, inside. Llew was the first person to make me feel like this, in fact my friends in Porthmadog loved to call me "the Ice-maiden". Now I felt fires leaping as Llew touched me: it was exciting, but a little frightening, too.

He released me then and helped Anja and Bernice Elkan to make sure everybody had plenty to eat. The Bulkeley family were shipping agents and ship owners, just like the Elkans, so they had met before, and had lots to talk about. Anja and her sister were asking, "What will happen in France, and in Russia?" Uncle Walter and Tada had arranged for the slates to be unloaded as quickly as possible, but there were many Welsh ships in the harbour, and with the various governments in Europe at one another's throats like wolves over a kill, we all felt unhappy, and uncertain of the future.

As soon as dusk fell we doused the fire and moved into the house, and there we had a real night to remember. Owen's first "grown-up" party and how he enjoyed it! Together with Guto and young Bobbo Elkan and his sisters they manned the bar, and served wine and beer to the older guests, and afterwards they retreated to the Den, and played charades.

I found myself with Llew – no, I must remember to call him Buck! – and Anja, Bernice, and their brothers Henk and Vincent. Ifor and Davy were with us too, but Peredur soon decided to join in the charades, getting to know the newest generation of young ladies, looking forward to future trips to Hamburg with slates, no doubt! You could see clearly how the intermix of friendships and marriages had come about over the last seventy years or so.

It was midnight before the party was over. We said goodnight to our friends, and Uncle Bob struggled to tell Nanna Elkan and all the ladies how much he had enjoyed the surprise. "Diwrnod i'r Brenin … [*a day for a king*]" he smiled. "A night to remember forever … "

Lots of the young people came with us down to the ship. Buck and I walked slowly, our arms intertwined, and were joined by two or three other couples. It was a night full of stars. I said "I feel as though we could just step onto the carpet of stars and ride the Milky Way all the way to heaven!" While everyone admired the lines of the new ship and the beauty of Nia's portrait, Owen was out on his feet. I took him below, and tucked him up in his berth. He hit the sack with his eyes tight shut almost before I could get his trousers off. "Diwrnod i'r Brenin, Rhian … " he echoed Uncle Bob, as he drifted away. I sang a few lines to him, but zonc! He was in the land of expectations!

It had been a wonderful, mind-shattering day for me too, and I didn't want it to end. I took a blanket, and curled up in the prow of the ship, next to Mam, and looked and dreamed. Tada was still on deck. I felt his eyes, warm and loving, caressing me.

"I hoped you'd remember her, cariad," he said. "I would never want you to forget her, and Marrion, my new wife, she wouldn't either. She belongs to the sea, too. In Labrador, in the Tickles they know the sea as we in Wales do. And they help each other through the sorrows, just as we do."

I looked at him, my eyes spurting tears. "It's lonely at sea, when you've no-one to come back to," he said. I tried to smile through the tears, "And its lonely at home, when you've no-one coming home to you … I love you so much Tada, make sure you come back to Nain and to me safely … and to Marrion, too. We'll wait for you forever … "

"What about Owen?" he started to say. I cut in "He'll be off with you as soon as he's old enough! … even I can see that!"

I woke as the sun came up, still curled up beside Mam. I think I like growing up!

We were ready to sail next day, expecting the steam tug to tow us out on the evening tide. Instead, we had only been asleep for two or three hours, when I felt some-one shaking me, to wake me up.

It was Tada, and he held a finger up to my mouth. "Quiet as possible, cariad," he whispered. He had arranged with Walter Elkan and several other friends that a steam tug would arrive to tow us out on the early morning tide.

When I got down to the galley I found Uncle Bob already there, with a breakfast of bread and butter, cold ham, and the fresh fruit we had loaded here in Hamburg, and surrounded by a crew of disgruntled, hung-over seamen already at the table. My surprise must have been obvious, for Uncle Bob started to explain to us, in Tada's absence, that just before the party ended last night word had come – quietly – that the enmity between Germany and Great Britain was coming to a head, and in the next day or two, war would be declared.

As a result, the shipping agents, and the pilots, for so many years friends of our families, had arranged tugs to take out on this early morning tide as many as possible of the little sailing ships. To be successful it must be done as quickly, and as quietly as possible, otherwise trouble could rebound on our long-time friends and their families.

So it was all hands on deck. Those vessels that were fully loaded, *Nia Ben Aur* among the first, fortunately for us, were towed down the Elbe, starting with the ships that had wives and children aboard.

We crept down the river, past the main harbour in Hamburg, which lay slumbering in these early hours.

As we reached down towards Cuxhaven, the moon was disappearing behind clouds, and a watery sun was emerging.

We heard later that not all the Welsh ships had got away. The *George Casson* was one Porthmadog ship that was still at the loading quay, and we wondered what had happened to her, and to Captain Bob Evans, Dafydd French, and the rest of her crew.

We did not even realise the danger our friends had put themselves in to save us, until we arrived in Plymouth, where we heard that war had been declared at eleven o'clock of the very morning of our escape, August the fourth.

Chapter Seven

We sailed across the North Sea as quickly as possible. Our course was not quite as straightforward as usual, as I over heard Tada explain to Owen. We sailed, using what wind there was, towards the English coast, and when we arrived in sight of Hartlepool, and only then, did we turn South, keeping as near as possible to the land. Our progress was slower, but safer, away from any enemy action.

Once more we were fortunate, as the seas were calm, and the wind steady behind us. All night long the whole of the crew, including Uncle Bob, Guto, and even Owen, split the watch between them. I'm not a very enthusiastic cook, nor an experienced one, but to free Uncle Bob for sailing duties, I ensconced myself in the galley, making sure everyone coming off watch had a hot meal and hot drink. It's strange, isn't it: while all we younger ones knew that Tada and Buck and Uncle Bob were really worried, for us it was a wild adventure. I don't think we felt anything could truly harm us.

All through the next day we hugged the coast line, from the Humber estuary, past the fenlands, till we were in sight of the Wash, and then, on through the darkness. By supper time, we were off the little port of Aldeburgh, and Tada gave orders for us to heave to. He himself had not slept since we left Hamburg, although we had prevailed upon him once or twice to rest on deck. Now he left Uncle Bob on watch, together with Peredur. They were to take two hours, while everyone else went below to sleep, or at any rate to lie in bed! After two hours of the dogwatch, Ifor and Davy would take over the watch, and a third dogwatch would bring Buck and Guto on watch. Owen was to be with them on deck, and if there was a favourable shift in the wind in that last two hours before midnight, we would all turn to, and make a dash for the white cliffs, and round the Kentish coast before daylight if possible. Needless to say, I peeped into Tada's cabin, and although he did sleep for a while stretched out on his bed, most of the time he spent checking his charts, making notes, writing up the log, with the occasional trip up on deck to check the weather, and the watch!

For the last watch before midnight he popped into my galley, and we prepared a good meal of hash, and salt beef, with carrots and the last of Nain's green beans. It was left in the oven to keep warm, and a good brew of tea was put ready.

Tada and I sat down to eat our helpings. " The tide will be full, about now, on the shore" he said, "and we'll get the sails up, and drift out a little way, and then softly, softly we'll get out to sea, clear of the shallows and the fishing banks, round the North Foreland, and past those cliffs by morning."

I felt *Nia Ben Aur* begin to rock gently, just as Tada had predicted, and looked at him. Just as I opened my mouth to say "Shall I go and see they are awake?", Tada took my hand. "Let Owen come and tell us, cariad." Three minutes later, Owen came scuttling in "Wind and tide getting lively, Captain. Shall I call all hands?" "I think we'll let Ifor and Davy have another hour of rest, but call the first watch, if you please, Owen. Well done young man!" I held a smile until Owen had gone to the foc'stle to call the others, and then I smiled "Well done, Captain, too!" I said cheekily, and then went and gave him an enormous hug.

Minutes later he was up on deck, and first Guto had his midnight feast, then Owen and Uncle Bob, and Peredur, and when they were all primed and I could feel Nia beginning her dance through the waves, Buck came down for his meal.

"I hear the supper is delicious," he said gravely. "Isn't that how the sirens of the ancient stories captured the hearts of young sailors? Should I beware?" He smiled at me; his eyes alight, as he teased. I felt myself blushing, and was glad to be able to cool my face with my hands, cold from the water butt.

He stood behind me, looking over my shoulder at the stove where the fire was burning. I had plaited my hair in a long plait, and then bound it round my head, the galley being such a small place, as I was afraid my hair would swing into the flames as I bent to the stove, and then turned quickly to put the food on the bench behind me. I felt Buck's hand stroking my hair. "It shines redder than the fire, in here", he whispered in my ear, bending close, "even tied up like now!"

Suddenly there was a clatter of shoes on the steps, and Ifor was standing in the doorway, yawning. "I felt the swell getting up, woke, and smelled the cooking … " he volunteered. His eyes shone, seeing the meat tin in the oven. "Smells good; Davy, grub's up!" he called.

Just as the mate and the two hands sat down to their food, Uncle Bob came, intending to call the two lads. "Oh, you're up, lads … " he started to say. But with a wink to the rest of us, Ifor said "It's good, my man. We'll pay you off at the next port. You will not be needed in the galley ever again! The new cook may not be an improvement on you in the cooking stakes, but merely the sight of her makes us all eager to work for ever and a day, aboard *Nia Ben Aur*!", added Davy, "and she's much prettier!" "Yes, it's time we sacked the old boy!" There was a moment of ghastly silence. I looked anxiously at Uncle Bob, who reached past me to the shelf where the salt, pepper, herbs and other flavourings were secured. Without so much as a wink or a grin he said "Oh, yes, Rhian fach, I see you used up all the sulphur and treacle in the gravy. That'll keep everyone on deck for tonight." Ifor and Davy pretended to look startled, and held on to their stomachs, and then we all burst into gales of laughter.

"Finish up here, my boys," grinned Uncle Bob, "and then Captain says we'll issue orders, all together on deck. Not too long, mind. It's a hard night ahead of us."

They all three ate up quickly, then, up on deck, me as well, Tada summed up our situation.

"We must pretend that this is a Clipper ship race," he suggested "I want four hands on watch, all the time, everyone else to jump to it, if called. Bob, you and I will go – now – and check the lifeboat. We'll check all the safety gear is aboard, plenty of fresh water, and Rhian, will you sort out some food and stow it on the ship's boat, not a great amount: we'll be fairly close inshore, but make it comforting, there's a good girl!" Buck took over the first watch, with Ifor, Guto and Uncle Bob. Second watch was Tada, Davy, Peredur and Owen. "When you are not on watch, go down below and rest, ready for the next session."

As we checked the lifeboat, Tada and Uncle Bob and me, the wind started to pick up strength, luckily blowing more or less south, the way we were heading. The tide too, was still running strongly. So much had happened since Tada and I had talked, that I was astounded to notice that it was still only 2 a.m. – lots of time to try to slip round the headland, and past those white cliffs. Tada was thinking, I realised, of the German invasion of Belgium, a week ago. If they had managed to outflank the French Defence lines, then we could be in real trouble. There had been so much talk of submarines, and Q-boats, and even aeroplanes, in these early years of the new century that it was hard to foretell what was going to happen.

Tada's voice rose, matching the dark velvet of the night sky.

> Yn y dyfroedd mawr a'r tonnau,
> Nid oes neb a ddeil fy mhen,
> Ond fy unig annwyl Iesu,
> A fu farw ar y pren.
> Cyfaill yw yn afon angau,
> Ef a'm dail yn uwch na'r don,
> Golwg arno wna i mi ganu
> Yn yr afon ddofn hon …

> *In the fierce seas and waves,*
> *There is no-one to hold my head,*
> *But my one and only dear Jesus,*
> *Who died on the Cross,*
> *He is a friend in the river of death,*
> *He holds me above the waters,*
> *One look at him makes me break into song,*
> *In the depths of this river …*

As he finished, he said, "That's it for now, my friends. As quiet as can be, till dawn … "

Chapter Eight

It took four more days and nights of hard sailing before we came within sight of Plymouth, where we would unload our small cargo of cattle food.

Tada went ashore at once, wondering what the turbulent future held for us all. He was gone for hours it seemed to us, anxiously waiting aboard ship. He came back on board in the agent's boat, and we were taken to our unloading berth, but it was quite clear that Tada's news was not good.

When the agents had gone, and we were tied up, ready to unload at dawn, he called us all below.

The war news was first: young men were being urged to join the army, and an Expeditionary Force of troops was ready to cross the channel to France.

"What do sailors do in wartime?" asked Owen.

"They sail the seas, and bring food and provisions to our people. It's very important for our families at home to have food, and materials for making guns, and uniforms", said Uncle Bob. "It's not just soldiers who win wars, you know!"

Then Tada said "I used the telephone in the office, to call the Mutual Society in Porthmadog, and they went to Chapel Street, to tell Nain we are all well, she will tell all your families at home. They brought Nain back with them, and from the Mutual Office, she spoke, to tell me that Marrion is ill, in Labrador. There is something wrong with the baby, and I want to work out some way to be there, with them."

"I think if I can get someone to take over command of *Nia Ben Aur*, then I can get across to Canada on a passenger liner." "You young ones had better go home, on the train to Porthmadog. Nain will come either to Liverpool or to Crewe to meet you, depending on the railway timetable."

Owen cut in "Why can't we sail home to Port, all of us together, Tada?" "I'm afraid that would take too long, Owen", Tada answered. "We must get to Cadiz for salt, and then to Labrador for fish. Salt fish is good food for times of war: it keeps well, it's tasty, and it gives you lots of energy.

The Mutual will let me know as soon as they find a qualified shipmaster, so I think you should all take a break while I do the organizing, for I'll be getting plenty of sleep on the steam ship while you are all sailing the Atlantic." With that we had to be content, and every one went below, except Uncle Bob, Owen and me.

I went to Tada and hugged him. "It will work out, you'll see. I have a good feeling about this trip." I said, and he smiled wanly at me.

"Get some sleep now, there's a good girl", and he gave me a lovely hug and a kiss. I couldn't sleep though, and so I sat and listened while Uncle Bob and Tada decided what must be done: there were extra stores to be taken aboard; the men of the crew to be warned to send home anything precious; letters to be written to their loved ones – just in case!

"I'm so worried for the young ones", I heard Tada say "Sailing the oceans is dangerous enough, without these new-fangled submarines, trying to sink us. I don't know what to do for the best, Bob, – whether to get them to Canada for the duration of this war, or to send them home to Porthmadog."

In the end, it was Owen who found the answer to Tada's dilemma. Uncle Bob had taken him and Guto for a wander around the harbour, while the cargo was being unloaded, next morning. They spotted a wooden barquentine – a three-master -, and the two lads didn't have to try too hard to persuade Choccy Bob to take them along to see it close up. As they stood admiring her lines, who should disembark but Finn Carlsen, who had carved *Nia Ben Aur*'s figurehead. "You'll have to come and see her" chanted Owen, and so, when the rest of the crew knocked off, to have a bite of dinner, Bob, Owen, Guto and Finn arrived to join us.

Finn told Tada that the "Endurance", for that was the ship, had left London on August the first, bound for Antarctica. When Captain Shackleton heard that war had been declared he brought the ship into Plymouth, to enquire whether the expedition could still go ahead. He thought the "Endurance", and the trained seamen and officers aboard her might be needed in Britain.

I was surprised to see Uncle Bob and the boys come back with reinforcements; I started to butter some more of the scones I had made while Uncle Bob was out of the way! Uncle Bob came aboard first. "Is the

Captain aboard, cariad?" he called. Tada appeared from below, at that point. "Problem solved!" crowed Uncle Bob. "See who we've brought!"

At that very moment the gaggle of young men appeared on the quay, alongside. Central among them, and the focus of all their fascination was Finn, who had carved our wondrous figurehead.

"Reporting for duty, Captain" he laughed. Tada gaped at him, and then they hugged one another, to my surprise. I knew they had sailed together, but I hadn't realised they were such good friends.

Owen cut in, "Captain Shackleton says he can come with us … "

"No, no, Finn bach," said Tada "you've wanted so much to go back there … There's me, thinking you were well on your way already! I heard you'd left London days ago."

"We are waiting, because of the war", said Finn …" It's possible we won't be going, and even if we do go, Captain Shackleton says I can join them at Buenos Aires, as he will do. I'll have time to sail '*Nia Ben Aur*' over to St John's first, and then get to Buenos Aires by October, or else South Georgia, where they expect to be until November."

That is how things were settled. Next day, Shackleton was told "Proceed", by Winston Churchill, at the Admiralty, and we all went along with Captain Shackleton and with Finn, to wave them God speed.

Chapter Nine

Tada was a different person. Suddenly, with Finn to take the ship to Newfoundland, he was making plans for the new baby, looking forward to seeing Marrion; I could not remember seeing him so happy for years.

I thought about going back home, but couldn't make up my mind. I could see, after just twenty four hours, that Owen would certainly not leave – at least, not until he was absolutely certain there was nothing more he and the youngsters could prise out of Finn, about Scott's journey, or Shackleton's new venture. Peredur, Guto, even Ifor and Davy, they had all written home with the exciting news, as proud as peacocks that they would be sailing with Finn as Captain.

I faced the fact: I had to choose between keeping Nain company, and looking after Owen. I wrote to Nain, and her reply came by telegram:

"You know you must look after Owen as you promised Nia, your mother, all those years ago. Enjoy your trip. Love Nain."

It must have cost her a small fortune. She had settled my doubts so quickly, that Tada was able to get away even sooner than he had dared to hope, and we waved him off on the train to Liverpool, from where he had a passage booked, even before we had loaded our cargo of railway sleepers for Cadiz.

Nia Ben Aur was quite beamy, and had a good capacity for cargo amidships for a small wooden sailing ship, although the lovely narrowed lines of her prow and stern disguised this and made her look more graceful than many of the old cargo carriers. I must admit that when they loaded the first of the lumpy, ugly sleepers, I ran below and wept, thinking of Mam. Somehow it seemed sadder than when we had loaded Ffestiniog slates; silly, I know, but the heavy timbers looked dark and threatening.

I looked up. Finn was quietly watching me. Almost like a thought reader he said. "They look ugly and threatening until you want to build a safe railway, and then each one can be a lifesaver. More use to man than gold or ivory." I smiled waveringly back at him.

He went on; "A bit like the sea: cold and threatening, or sparkling with promise, depending on us really." Suddenly, and for no reason, sadness and uncertainty plunged me into floods of tears. He held me tight in his arms, just as Tada would, and he cradled my head on his heart, and just held me while I wept. I thought I heard Mam's lullaby for a moment "Cwsg yn dawel, annwyl blentyn ... " [*sleep at peace, dearest child*], but there came a noisy hooting of passing ships jockeying for leeway, and all the banging of heavy cargoes, and the furious noise of a busy dock, drowning out the far-off voice.

Finn loosed his hold of me, and smiled in his quiet way. "Popeth yn iawn, rŵan? [*Everything all right now*]" and as I smiled shakily, he shot away up the gangway, and I heard him checking the hatches.

Two days later we had taken aboard all our stores and provisions, as well as the cargo, and we were off to Cadiz. I stood beside Buck as we sailed out. It was early morning, and somehow it struck me that we were sailing west, away from the warmth of the sun, as it rose behind us in the east. So different from the way I had felt as we sailed westwards into the sunset, when we left Porthmadog – when was that – just weeks ago. It seemed that my life had stretched under so much strain, in between.

The wind was behind us, and we fairly raced along. Strange really, the fact that iron ships were replacing our wooden hulls that danced along on the top of the waves. Iron is so heavy; you would think it would be a handicap – and yet, because the turbines drive the ships along, they are able to keep the hull water-tight in bad weather. I couldn't help thinking it might be a much uglier world in a hundred years' time.

I went along to help Uncle Bob in the galley. Everything was under control, as usual, and he said "You get yourself out with the lads" – "efo'r hogiau" were his exact words, in Welsh. "A voyage West, is always something to be savoured", he scolded me. I gave him an enormous kiss, right on top of his bald patch "Yes, Friar Tuck" and skipped out of reach very quickly.

While we were in the dangerous waters of the coastline Finn had decided to stick with Tada's system of four on, four off, watches, and now Finn himself was at the wheel, Davy was busy in the wheelhouse, and Peredur was clearly checking the spars and the rigging, making everything shipshape – not a sign of Owen! Panic started to take the air out of my lungs ... and at that very moment Finn shifted ever so slightly, and I spied at the wheel a small figure – Owen, at the helm, – and memory jogged at me – just as Tada had stood behind me as we sailed the seas, long long ago. I seem to remember we were striking out for home from ... I couldn't tell where, and the more I tried the less I recalled. So I took my place now, in the bow, beside Mam's figurehead, and dreamed, until it was time to think about something to eat.

And so the days passed; I envied Owen his freedom to be one of the crew. He and Guto learned to climb about in the rigging safely, to take the helm, to navigate. Every day they learned a new shanty; "Ranso was a schoolboy", "Beware of the black velvet band"; Uncle Bob was responsible for most of those, I think, and then when darkness fell, watch by watch they came for a good hot supper.

The pattern of our days was already set by the time we reached Cadiz, where we unloaded our sleepers, and loaded up, with eighty last of salt, for delivery to St John's, Newfoundland. We set sail on the 23rd of August, grateful not to have to go to Gibraltar, nor into the Mediterranean, where we were told that German U-boats were creating havoc.

Finn needed to use the Captain's cabin, as much of the equipment was stored in safety there, so I had suggested that he and Buck should share its use, while I had the mate's cabin. We set out from Cadiz at a great rate of knots, with a following wind, blowing strongly but steadily. The prevailing winds are more usually from the west, so that the journey back home is regularly faster than the voyage out to Canada, so we felt that at last good fortune might be on our side. As the days passed the crew gradually became a team. Finn, Uncle Bob, Ifor and Davy had sailed together before. Peredur, too, had served on *Olwen* for her last voyages, but Buck, Guto and Owen and I, were an unknown quantity. As I soon learned, there is no better way to become a family – or not! – than in a small working sailing ship.

Before we left Cadiz, Finn brought us all together. Uncle Bob and I had been ashore and bought as much fresh fruit and vegetables as we could hope to eat before they spoiled. We had a selection of tapas, enchilladas, and lobster fritters, and a grand paella in the oven, for this last Spanish supper, and we all sat down to eat.

With the cheese, which followed, Finn poured us all a glass of Madeira wine – just a small glass for the boys and for me, of course. He stood up and proposed a toast.

"My friends let us drink to the health of the seamen of Porthmadog, and their families." We all raised our glasses, and smiled at one another as we drained our delicious wine. It tasted like rich velvet as it slid down my throat, as smooth as satin, leaving a glow, which kept my whole body warm.

"Our orders are to make for St. John's, Newfoundland, to see where we must unload our cargo of salt. Because of the danger from enemy U-boats, and warships and the rest, we must be doubly watchful. It's not only the winds, the rain, and the ocean that we have to look out for, this voyage."

Finn went on, "I'm going to suggest two watch teams, but if anyone can think of a better, safer way, shout up at once."

I don't know if it was the Madeira wine speaking, but we all "Aye-ayed" blissfully.

"I think, perhaps, myself, Davy, Guto and Owen, who tells me he wants to be one of the crew – one of us – not a passenger!"

"For the second team, you must be in charge, Buck, with Ifor and Peredur to support you."

I cut in "What about me?" There was a hush of embarrassment.

"I think you want to remember all the women who have been sailors! Grace Darling … "

Luckily, because my mind had gone blank with anguish, and I couldn't think of another heroine of the seas, Finn interrupted.

"I see what you mean, Rhian, and I think you are quite right" he said, "but the word had to come from you."

I smiled cheekily at him, as he went on.

"I had thought about the situation," and he looked sideways at me, just as Tada always did, "remembering that Satan finds work for idle hands … " he grinned fiendishly at me, "So my idea is that you, Rhian, and Bob, should share the work in the galley."

At this I pulled a long face, but he had not finished, "and that will leave you both with some time on your hands to help with the watches. The other way would be for one of you to be the cook, and the other join the watch teams."

He was surprised, and puzzled by the outburst which followed. "I said we'd get you out of the galley, old timer," joked Davy, and all the rest added their twopennorths.

"You be careful, now," Uncle Bob quipped. "There's plenty of squills and paragoric left"

"It might be worth it" Buck cut in, "The new chef is getting lovelier by the minute, with all this sunshine and sea air!"

"Gwenithen y genethod ... [*the golden choice among the girls*]", Peredur smiled shyly at me.

"I think your first idea will suit Uncle Bob and me best", I said to Finn, graciously condescending, a bit like old Queen Victoria "and the rest of you too."

So it was decided: when we had finished in the galley I would spend the extra time with Buck, on his watch, while Bob helped with Finn's watch. Better him than me to keep an eye on Guto and Owen, I thanked the stars.

Buck hadn't been looking too impressed with Finn's ideas at first, but when I volunteered to join his group, his face spoke volumes, and yet again we stayed quite late wondering at the beauty of the stars, on this our last night in port.

The next morning, as we slid out of the harbour on the tide, Captain Finn, as the boys had christened him, was on watch, with Davy, Uncle Bob, and the boys, but I must admit that the whole crew were on deck as we left. As Ifor remarked, "If I was a U-boat captain I'd be waiting outside Cadiz for the ships setting off on the tide, for Newfoundland."

"Luckily", said Bob, "they haven't got enough U-boats to watch all the ports. I should think Gibraltar will be the number one target hereabouts."

"Yes, 'cause they'll be watching for the ships coming through the Med, from Patras and Genoa."

We were fortunate. Guto and Owen had decided to practise climbing the rigging. Suddenly, from above,

"Captain, there's a warship right off the coast, towards Corunna," sang Guto.

"You're sure?" Finn looked up.

"Yes", came from Owen "honest, cross my heart. No joking."

We all went about our tasks as silently as possible, as the minutes ticked past. Then, "It's one of ours." "She's showing us her ensign", came from the two boys, like the chorus in an operetta. We all relaxed again.

Uncle Bob and I were halfway through preparing breakfast, anyway. Bacon and scrambled eggs, with hashed ship's biscuit tossed in the bacon fat – yummy! The bacon wouldn't keep for long on board ship, so it was a special treat.

Finn stayed on watch, with the boys to help him, while all the rest of us ate our breakfast, and then Davy took over, with Bob, while Finn, Guto and Owen joined us.

Chapter Ten

By this time it was eight bells, and time for our watch to take over. "Will you wash up, and tidy away, Uncle Bob?" I asked. "I'll go on deck with Ifor, Peredur and Buck as it's our watch."

"Great", Finn replied on behalf of Uncle Bob, who was already piling up the dirty dishes, to be fair.

As I joined the other on deck, I heard Finn's voice, "You two lads still look pretty lively. You can come down to the cabin, and we'll decide how we're going to outwit all these enemies, and get to St. John's."

The boys' eyes shone with excitement as they followed him eagerly below.

"He's good with the young ones, isn't he" remarked Ifor.

"If it had been left with you, Buck, or me, we'd be treating them like kids, and they'd be as sick as a couple of penguins by now."

"It's not as though he has family of his own, either", agreed Peredur.

"I think it's something Finn's picked up from his voyages with Tada" I said. "He's so like Tada sometimes, it's almost uncanny."

Buck looked delighted, but there were raised eyebrows from the other two.

We soon fell into a routine. The constant watch made it easier in some ways: there was no time for arguments or anything like that.

We found that the shorter dog-watches made it easier for Uncle Bob and me to share the work in the galley, and third day out Finn called some of us into the cabin.

"What do you think about splitting the four till eight watches, both for breakfast, and for supper in the evening, as well? That way it's easier for Rhian and you, Bob, to share the work in the galley for both main meals. You can concentrate on watch, without worrying about how things are cooking below."

Bob and I both nodded in appreciation, but there were some doubts voiced.

"It might be easier, and more regular, if Bob did the galley, and Rhian became permanently one of my watch … " Buck started to say.

Finn cut in "It would also mean that we could share the remaining watches so that the two growing boys can get some sleep at night."

"It's quiet, from midnight until four o'clock in the morning. Davy and I can manage most of the time, between the two of us, with Bob to help, giving Guto and Owen a little more time in their bunks. But it would mean you would always have the sunset to midnight, Buck, which is usually busier, especially with the war on."

He put the idea to the vote, unknown to Guto and Owen, of course. They would have been mortified to think they were being eased into their bunks!

"Carried", said Finn gladly, and in the morning I got the job of explaining to the lads, without upsetting them.

"You two can't come off watch, and just jump into bed, like the rest of us," I put it. "After all, you are apprentice seamen, and even in wartime you have to do your studies. Tada made Finn promise!"

It worked very well. Owen was delighted to be officially an apprentice, however temporary his status!

Over the next few days the wind was behind us, and we skipped along. The steam driven ships tended to follow pre-set courses, but we tended to make our own routes, every journey a variation on a theme. When the winds and the storms beat at sailing ships, a trip from Cadiz to St. John's might take ten weeks or more, but with the steady but strong breeze in our sails, we were making very good time.

It constantly amazed me that boys – well, young men – who had grown up in such similar environments could end up so different.

Ifor and Davy had grown up almost in one another's pockets. They were from two families who live in New Street, in Porthmadog. Ifor was a year older, and he was married to Davy's twin sister. They went to the same Chapel, to the same School.

Ifor was shy, lacking in confidence in himself, though with no good reason, for he was very good indeed at his work. He could have gone to college to gain his Master's ticket, but he was waiting for Davy to be qualified to go too, so that they could be together. His excuse was that he had not wanted to be at college when his first son was born.

Davy was not married. The first time I remember seeing him, he was still at school, and he was on the school roof, walking along it from end to end with no support at all. He always loved the circus that came on Bank Holiday Monday, in the summer, and for a short time he ran away, and performed as an acrobat and tumbler, with them. He didn't like seeing the animals trained, though. He wasn't quite as good at the written work as Ifor, but he was superbly fit.

Peredur, like Finn, didn't miss anything in the scenery around about. He wasn't from a farming and sailing background, like the others. The surprising thing about Peredur was that he loved ideas, words. He wrote poetry and songs, and he was a very fine painter, too. He often spent his leisure time on the quayside, painting the harbour scenes, in water-colour.

Guto, even at his tender age, was an engineer in the making. He saw at a glance how things should work, and he was tremendously successful at repairing any gadgets that went wrong.

Owen was a natural "Bossy-boots". He was bright and intelligent, and unlike Guto and Peredur, he was not slow to voice his opinions – usually in a very loud voice, at that!

Buck was different, but then he had been born into a wealthier family altogether. Yes, for me Buck was definitely special.

The eight till midnight watch, which Buck was in charge of, was my favourite time at sea. The sun would be setting in the west, where the sky shone and sparkled like shot silk. Later the moon would come up, and all the multitude of stars.

One such night, when it was almost midnight, Ifor and Peredur were at the helm, while Buck and I had moved into the wheel-house. Buck's voice came from the darkness,

"Rhian, when you stand, outlined against the sky like that, with the moon beyond your shoulders, you are the most beautiful woman of my dreams!"

"Buck!" I gasped, "Ifor and Peredur will hear you."

"Let them" said Buck. "They all know I've fallen in love, even if you have not noticed!"

He smiled, leaning over me, holding me close. I felt his heart thumping.

We stayed, close together, until midnight, when Uncle Bob came up, purposefully whistling. I got the feeling that he was warning of the approach of the new watch. Owen would be with them, so I eased myself out of Buck's arms.

The young ones, Owen and Guto, had not as yet welcomed Buck into their gang, and I didn't want Owen to feel that Buck was coming between us.

We went below, and drank the mugs of tea left for us, and I loosened the tight braids of my hair. As he helped me to the Mate's cabin, which should, of course have been his, Buck's hands smoothed my hair and stroked my back. I shivered with joy as I felt him, and reached up. Holding his head between my hands, I drew him down, and kissed him longingly on his lips.

We clung to one another for long, luscious minutes, and then, a little surprised at myself, I turned and ran into the cabin.

I lay in bed. Young ladies didn't do things like that. Only bad girls kissed young men before they were married – or at least promised in marriage, I scolded myself. And yet what I felt in my heart was a singing happiness, turning my whole world into paradise and I cwched down, in my pyjamas, and dreamed myself into sleep.

After that, the eight to midnight watch was the high point of the day, for me. I found myself showing the best of me to the world. It was as if my happiness spilled over, to embrace the whole ship, and her crew.

The moon deserted us at the end of that second week, but the darkened skies meant that our progress was safer. Buck and I still finished the night watch together, and I got closer to Ifor and Peredur, during the earlier hours.

Ifor talked to me about his life with Davy's sister, and I tried my very best to convince him that among the community in Porthmadog he was considered a very fine seaman, certain to be master of a ship one of these days.

He had a little boy, and a new baby daughter, and we planned what we would take home to little Ios and for Cerys, and too for Morfudd, his wife.

Davy and Morfudd, the twins, had been very close when they were young.

"Lots of my school friends envied her, because Davy took her climbing, sailing and fishing, instead of treating her as just a girl, leaving her to look after the geese and the ducks, and feed the hens, and scrub the kitchen" I said. "Girls are growing up different: we want more from life now."

Peredur cut in "Do you think that goes for Jenny, too?"

"For sure!", I said. "If you want Jenny to love you, you must take her up Cnicht, Tryfan, and follow the hounds' run up Rhyd-ddu to Snowdon; you must sail with her on Llyn Cwellyn … "

"Instead of love songs and poems?" poor Peredur looked crestfallen.

"Not instead of – as well as!" I amended, seeing his misery.

"Especially for Jenny. She loves poetry and poets of course. Well, we all do, Rhiannon as well. Only she likes her words set to music!" I managed to get a relieved smile from Peredur, at last.

"Jenny and I, we'll both be going next year to Coll" I said "I hope you'll come up to Bangor to see us when you're in port. Buck says he'll come, so you'll have company."

We were brought down to earth. The two youngsters were coming up the companionway chanting,

> Un, dau, tri,
> Mam yn dal pry',
> Pry' wedi marw,
> Mam yn crio'n arw …
>
> *One, two, three,*
> *Mother caught a flea,*
> *The flea died,*
> *Mother cried and cried …*

It took me half an hour to realise they hadn't found any fleas! They were getting their own back on me for all my teasing.

Chapter Eleven

We were sixteen days out of Cadiz by this time, and running not more than a day or so behind the best time on record made by a schooner. That night, Guto and Owen, under Finn's supervision, had worked out that as we had covered almost three thousand miles, we ought now to be on the look out for the shallows and banks off the Newfoundland coast.

The moonlight that night was brilliant. *Nia*'s sails shone ghostly silver as we slid through a lovely dark blue sea. I stood in the stern just before we went below to sleep, and we were gliding through the waves like a fairy ship. In our wake the moonbeams flickered on the plankton like a myriad of drowning stars, or a path of diamonds leading the way to Paradise.

At midnight, Finn appeared on deck, ready to take over the watch. This time, he had not only Davy but the two youngsters, awake and lively this night, eager to watch for signs of the New World. In a way, it must have been just as thrilling for them as for Eric the Red, long ago – well perhaps for Leif Ericson, or Eric's grandsons, at any rate!

Uncle Bob was bringing up some toffee he and I had made for the occasion. Not treacle toffee, like Nain's 'cyflaith', but we had decided that as we had made such good time, we could spare a couple of tins of condensed milk; it makes really sweet chewy toffee.

It was such an exciting time that Buck, Ifor, Peredur and I hung around on deck, and it was long enough before we retired to our berths.

When I awoke, just two or three hours later, the moon had disappeared, and not a star remained in the whole of the heavens. The sky gradually lightened to a dark, muddy shade of grey, but there was no sign of the sun, to greet us.

The wind was growling in the shrouds, and in the few moments on deck, until I shot below, to make a warming meal for the foursome on watch, the wind swung round, to hit us from the North West. The two boys were struggling to reef the gaffsails. Guto had long ago worked out that he and Owen, working together, could do everything that the older, stronger men could achieve. He had shown Owen that by making an angle, a sort of corner, in the ropes they were working, their pull was vastly increased. This was the method they were using now, but the wind was so wild and shifting so capriciously, that they were in danger of being blown over, and although they were wearing belts, they might well be injured.

Fortunately, Ifor and Peredur were appearing on deck, and managed to give Finn a hand. Davy was already struggling to hold the wheel steady, as the wind and the waves beat at *Nia Ben Aur*.

The Grand Banks are always dangerous; the worst storm tracks in the northern hemisphere seem to converge there. For the next six hours, we fought not to be driven all the way North and back east, to Greenland or Iceland.

Finn had sent the younger members of the crew below. There was still plenty of work for us to do, packing away everything that might crash, and cause cuts, or broken bones, making sure the lasts of salt in the cargo did not break loose.

On deck, Finn himself, Buck, Ifor, Davy and Bob wrestled with the constantly changing wind patterns, the tumultuous waves, which *Nia* climbed, and then raced down, each time threatening never to surface again.

Around mid-day, we gave thanks to God. The winds dropped a few knots, and the height of the waves became frightening, rather than stupefying, a mere thirty feet.

I had everything ready to feed the whole crew, in relays. It was cold food, since to have kept the fire burning would have been dangerous, but I had done the best I could – pilfered all Uncle Bob's secret hidey-holes where he kept birthday treats. They all agreed that I'm very good at opening cans of bully beef, pineapple chunks, and tins of sweet biscuits.

The lull lasted for fully ninety minutes, and then just as we were thinking about re-lighting the fire under the oven, in the galley, the pitch of the deck increased again, and we were back out of the eye of the storm.

It was eight long, anxious hours before the storm finally abated, and we could start to make everything shipshape once more, while Finn and Buck tried to decide how far off our course we had been driven and how best to head back.

It took us five more days to get back within sight of the Newfoundland coast, and then *Nia Ben Aur* was becalmed for a further twenty-four hours. Work as we might, and with journey's end so near, we could have walked faster, on the water!

As we approached the land, late in the day, Finn had offered a treat to whomever spotted land first. Owen and Guto were up on the top gallant yard, determined to be joint winners.

"Who do you think first landed here in the New World?" Buck had asked them, before they went aloft.

"Eric the Viking" was Davy's answer.

"St. Brendan" from Ifor.

"Prince Madog" from Peredur

"The Indians", from Bob, the "The Inuit" from Finn.

"Who were they?" I asked, mystified.

"Eskimos", Finn smiled at me.

At that point, two young voices sang out jointly, from aloft, "Land Ho".

As we sailed on towards St. John's, the moon rose in the sky, a reminder of the wonderful nights of the early voyage. Buck stood beside me, as we gazed westward. In some ways, I didn't want the voyage to end. We were so happy, so much in love, Buck and me. He slid his arm round my waist and hugged me close to him.

Vaguely, I heard Finn directing the young ones. "The first light we see should be Cape Spear. Look out for the flash from the lighthouse. You may find it a little to the South of where we expect it: that's because we were blown adrift to the North, when the storm came … "

Guto's voice cut in "There she is" and at almost the same instant, "Light ho!" from Owen, his delight rippling in his cry.

Finn swung the helm to head us along the shore, and I began to wonder how things had gone, with Marrion and the baby. Whether Tada would be in St. John's to meet us – but no, that couldn't be, I thought, he wouldn't know when we would have made landfall.

We beat our way against the wind, yet again, towards the shore for an hour or more. The two boys were looking mystified as Finn took us in towards an unbroken line of cliffs. Owen, always quicker to question than Guto, cried out, "Can't you see where we're going, Captain Finn?" an anxious tremor in his voice.

"No more than you can, Owen. Well spotted, young man." There was a smile in Finn's voice now.

"Never be afraid to question," and then, as if he'd waved a wand, out of the background of rockfaces and towering pine woods, we sailed round to view the narrows, and into the gauntlet that is the entrance to St. John's.

"There's another light flashing. Is that Fort Amherst?" Owen asked. I suspect, mind, that Guto deliberately let him get in first with the identification!

To our port side, we saw an enormous headland, with a light flashing, from the lighthouse on a craggy outcrop below.

To starboard Uncle Bob pointed out Signal Hill where Marconi's first telegraph message was received from far across the Atlantic Ocean, just a few years before.

It was growing dark by this time, and Captain Finn decided to drop an anchor, and to wait for the pilot to take us in when the sun came up.

In the meantime, "Well done, Guto, Well done Owen, too," Finn congratulated them both, and instructed Uncle Bob to fish two shiny sixpenny bits out of the kitty.

"What's more, I think all you men have done brilliantly, this voyage," Finn went on. "I think you should each have a shilling, something in your hands when we get ashore in the morning. I think you'll find there is enough in the box, Bob". Finn had obviously intended to give them a little bonus, all along. Even I got my shilling.

Uncle Bob had been coming here over the years, and as the sun went down he pointed out to Peredur, Guto, Owen and Buck and me, all clustered at the bow of *Nia Ben Aur*, the myriad dangers which threaten ships entering St. John's.

"Up yonder, on Signal Hill, is Cabot Tower, and you will see the Battery, below, once the sun comes up, in the morning", I heard him say. "They'll have all the big guns manned, with this war on" he added.

I left them all, in the end, and went down to get a little celebration supper, and when I came back up on deck Uncle Bob was still regaling the newcomers with tales of the Wash Balls, where a friend of his father, from Liverpool, had come a cropper. He had stories about all the hazards facing ships entering the Narrows: passing Chain Rock and

Pancake Rock, the names tripped off his tongue.

"Uncle Bob can't have been here when *all* those disasters happened", I puzzled.

"No, cariad," Ifor grinned at me. "Bob's not a great drinker, as you know, but when he gets ashore he meets up with all the old salts, over a glass of beer, and they swap stories all night!"

After we had eaten, as we sat in the moonlight on deck, I could have believed that we had been spirited back across the ocean to the wooded inlets of Cumbria or Scotland, except that everything seemed larger than life. The trees – fir, pine, maples, – were huge; the cliffs were gigantic, only the full moon seemed the same one that shone on us at home in Porthmadog.

Ifor gave me his glasses to see more clearly, and I noticed the huge guns, at Fort Amherst, trained on the ships waiting, like us, to enter the harbour.

"I've not seen those guns before", said Ifor, "but let's hope they'll never be needed to sink German warships trying to come in here."

We were all tired, and fell asleep in our bunks, except for Davy, who was on watch.

In the morning, the pilot boarded, and his steam tug took us in to the quayside, where we tied up; and after the usual customs checks, we could go ashore.

Uncle Bob took charge of Guto, Owen and me, and took us by tram-car – street-cars they call them here, – to Quidi Vidi Lake, and up Signal Hill. We met his friends on the water front, the Whiteleys, Captain Murray and his friends the Earles. We unloaded our cargo of salt, over several days, and then it was time to sail "down North", as they say here, to Rainbow Tickle, where Tada would be waiting for us.

We were all dying to hear his news, and to see him again.

Chapter Twelve

Tada was waiting for us on the quay. As we sailed in, we saw him, and waved madly, and he set away a great kite, shaped like an eagle. With him we could see a lady – too young, I felt sure, to be our new mother, Marrion. The houses crouched round the harbour wall looking down into the sea like mourners into a grave.

We moored, and as we had come only from St. John's, we were spared the customs men, and the effort to tie up where we could unload. In fact, Tada waved us to a mooring, which he had clearly kept for us; and we found that it was directly below Marrion's home, which was called the Eagle's Nest.

It was Cathy beside him, as we found when Owen and I rushed to hug him. She is Marrion's daughter, and we had seen a photograph of her as bridesmaid, at the wedding, of course; but now she looked more grown up, prettier, but rather shy.

Marrion and Cathy's father had been married for eight years before he died, and since then Marrion had run the smallholding on her own, until Cathy was old enough to help. The fishing boat had been taken over by her husband's two brothers, but they shared any profits they made with her.

Tada told us about his journey to join his new family. When he arrived he had found Marrion having to rest in bed, because she was in danger of losing her baby prematurely. Her sisters-in-law were looking after the farm, and Cathy was looking after her mother, and the household.

They were fortunate, for Tada had travelled on the steam ship with two nurses, who were on their way from Scotland to work in Dr. Grenfell's hospital, in Battle Harbour, and he persuaded the family to head that way, for their next fishing trip, and to take Tada and Marrion to the hospital straight away. The outcome was that they had these two darling little twins, and although they were small as yet, they and Marrion, too, were making great progress, and had been allowed to come back home, to everyone's delight.

We went to the house. Marrion greeted us with a kiss. She was out of her bed, and in the kitchen. The cradles were there, and Owen and I, after a quick hug, dashed to see the babies. They were nothing like one another: we couldn't help laughing! One was cwched up, shyly, and the other – the littlest one – even now, at three or four weeks of age, was looking at everything – sizing us up!

They had little woolly outfits, and the first thing I did was to get out all the presents we had brought. The presents from Porthmadog were first, and then the ones from Hamburg. "I thought at the time that it was a pity to have two of everything – one Welsh, one German – but it's just as well, isn't it!" I laughed.

By now, it was dinnertime, and I helped Cathy to set the table. Marrion's sister, who lived near-by, was there to help with a meal.

The kitchen was remarkably like home: a long room, full of sunshine, a cheerful fireplace, and in the middle, a big solid wooden table. We soon learned that because of the forests, wooden doors, floors, stairs, and all the furniture were beautiful, and all the ladies were very proud of them. Marrion said this table had been her grandma's, and it had clearly been loved and polished – cherished for her sake as well as its own, and the same was true of the bench seat by the wall, and the eight chairs round the table.

The sun poured in from the long window; making the waves glitter like sapphires set in silver, and *Nia Ben Aur*'s masts tossed their heads in the sunshine. We couldn't see our figurehead, which was just below the line of the quay. We were amused to notice several young boys, and some old salts, admiring her, and chatting with Uncle Bob and the others. They were obviously old friends.

There was a flagpole, too, and Tada had fastened the kite to the top, where the Earle's Fisheries flag flew, and underneath we saw Y Ddraig Goch [*the Red Dragon of Wales*], and the Union Jack, and another flag. "What's that one?", asked Owen. "The Finnish flag, for Finn, of course", said Tada.

Uncle Bob saw us at the window and waved. Marrion's voice came from where she stood behind me. "Bob's still with you, then and Finn's back from the other end of the world!"

"When we sold *Olwen* I persuaded Jack Beynon to stay with her", said Tada. "He was ready to master his own ship, and I took on young Bulkeley. But he hasn't got his master's ticket yet, and we were lucky to find Finn, when I heard you were ill, sweetheart."

I turned and smiled at my new Mam, and she smiled back, and pulled me close.

The days passed too quickly; there was such a lot to see and do. From the first day Cathy had taken a shine to Buck, and he was a bit uncomfortable, but I said "Don't be unkind to her, Buck. It must be very lonely for her, out here and she's obviously never met anyone like you before ... ." So Cathy showed us around, Buck and me, and sometimes Owen, while Tada and Finn, who had both been here before, organized the cargo of salt fish, to be shipped home.

"You must come over with Tada when this horrid war is finished, and meet all the family and friends ... " I said "Everyone will want to see you, and the babies."

Tada had written to Nain, but with submarines and all the dangers, we couldn't know yet that she had got the letter. Marrion is tall, and strong. She and Cathy had long jet-black hair. It was straight, and so shining and heavy that it was like velvet, so that you always wanted to stroke it.

Cathy loved to wash her hair and then brush it dry in the sunshine, especially when Buck was there to watch. Once Owen and I came back from a trip to see the seals on the rocks, and Buck was standing brushing it for her. Owen started to laugh, but I covered his mouth with my hand quickly. Cathy was so small, unlike her tall mother, and sometimes could look very lost and sad: it made us all want to look after her, and protect her.

We didn't see all that much of Finn because he was busy telling all the local lads about the Antarctic expedition, and that kept Owen busy, too.

Sad as we would be to leave the Eagle's Nest, we had to push on as soon as the Twinks – as Uncle Bob had christened them – had been christened officially! They were named after the two ladies who had embroidered their christening gowns: Sarah, after Nain, and Rosa, after Nanna Elkan. They behaved beautifully, too: cried vigorously to frighten the devils away, and then smiled beatifically!

We had a firework party, to finish the day. Cathy liked to sing, so I taught her some Welsh songs, and we sang some Canadian and

American songs, too. We were both surprised to find that "Pen Rhaw", was the tune of the American Stars and Stripes. Cathy was ready to retreat into her shell when Owen said "She's not as good a singer as Rhiannon, is she". But when I explained that Rhiannon had been selected for training as an opera singer, she was quite pleased, after all.

Buck's no musician, but Tada, Finn, Uncle Bob, Owen and I sang Pennillion for them, with Ifor playing the harmonica, as there was no harp.

We had loaded a part cargo of salt cod, and now we called at two other small villages on the sea's edge, for more salt fish. Each time Owen and I watched the cod being cured, and laid out on the flakes, as the cargo was loaded by the lads of the crew.

Finally, we collected a deck cargo of timber, which had been brought down from the sawmills. The deals were lashed down with ropes, balanced on either side of the deck. They made *Nia Ben Aur* look a little ungainly, but timber was desperately needed in Britain, and trade with the European countries was becoming very difficult.

It had been a tearful farewell, when we left the Eagle's Nest. Cathy wept, as she threw kisses to Buck, and Tada looked full of grief as he left Marrion, and he waved to the Twinks, who were being held up at the kitchen window by Marrion's sister, and sister-in-law.

The local lads waved goodbye to Finn, to Ifor and Davy and Uncle Bob, who they remembered from earlier visits, and to Owen, Peredur and Guto, their new friends. Owen almost disgraced himself with a few tears! Uncle Bob was on hand as we sailed off on the tide, with a picnic tea of partridgeberry pancakes, the berries brought from St. John's.

Chapter Thirteen

By Friday we were out beyond Newfoundland, and the weather was getting worse. Evening came, as we were off Cape Race. The wind was wild, gusting and then dropping, and wheeking in the rigging as if to remind us all of the two little ones left behind. The timbers on the deck had changed the shape of *Nia Ben Aur*, and instead of dancing along on the crest of the waves, the wind, as it hit the piles of planks, made her leap forward and then plough down into the depth of each breaker.

She was shipping a lot of water. All hands were on deck. Buck was standing by the ship's boat, and Uncle Bob was in charge of Guto, Owen and me, while Tada and Finn, together with the rest of the men waited for the right moment to cut the timbers loose.

Everything happened at once. Davy was at the helm, keeping her head up into the wind, when suddenly, from nowhere, and without any forewarning, a huge squall hit us. Tada shouted "Get the young ones aboard, and cut the lifeboat loose, Buck!", and just as the boat hit the water, seeing that we were not aboard, he called "Look after the kids, Finn", and in the same breath, "We'll see to the timber, and then every man for himself."

By the time he got the last words out, Nia was heeling over, but the timbers, as they broke loose, tipped her upright again. For a flash, it seemed she would hold her course, but she was deep in the waves, weighed down by the water she had shipped, and under our very feet she slid away.

Finn dived for me, and held me tight. Uncle Bob reached for Owen, but the two boys, Owen and Guto slithered away, blown by the wind. They cannoned head over heels, right over the rail. As soon as I got my breath, I screamed for someone to help them, Finn thrust me into Bob's grip, and was over the side, after them.

The whole ship capsized, in the raging whirlpool, and seemed to turn over on top of him. From above, lighting flashed like burning wire, and I was in the water.

Uncle Bob and I struck out for clear water, and gripped a plank.

Uncle Bob pushed me on to it, while he reached for another, and then we used my leather belt to lash them together. Ifor had seen us; he trailed some of the rope he had cut to jettison the deals when the storm broke, and we were able to lash two more planks to our raft.

At that moment, I spotted figures, clinging to another plank. Finn had managed to reach the two young ones just as we had seen the ship heel on to them. Now, he hailed us, and we managed to haul them up onto our tiny raft of planks. Finn shouted, over the storm, "Owen is hurt. Take a look and tie his foot up", and then he dived down again.

We hauled Guto and Owen on to the planks, and I hugged Owen close. His face was ashen white, and he was struggling for breath. Uncle Bob pinched his nose, and started pushing his chest gently, and then Owen wrenched his head sideways and spewed out a stomachful of water and rubbish. His eyes blinked, over and over. Then just as he caught sight of me and heard my voice, he smiled a sideways sort of smile, his hand gripped tight, tight, on to mine.

I smiled back at him, and Uncle Bob said "Takes more than the Atlantic Ocean to keep a good man down, eh, Owen."

Owen grinned wanly.

I reached for his shirt, where there were smears of blood, but Uncle Bob held my hand, saying "One thing at a time, cariad."

Uncle Bob had helped Guto to get back his breath while I saw to Owen, and Ifor held the raft together. Guto's ribs looked red and sore, but they did not seem to be crushed, and now we started to look around again for the rest of the crew.

We saw a figure burst out of the rolling waves, and once more it was Finn. We all reached out to help, and pulled Finn and Davy to the raft. One glance told us that Davy's life was over: he had been battered by the deals as they gathered momentum on their drop into the ocean.

Again and again, Finn dived under the ship. He would not give up. Buck, Peredur and Tada were not accounted for as yet. We scanned the waves for a sight of the lifeboat, but by now it was dark. Even the stars seemed to have deserted us.

Bob and Ifor tried to argue with Finn, but he said there was still a pocket of air in the below deck, and next time, he came up with someone in his arms. He waved frantically for one of us to help, and Ifor was diving into the rollers before any of us could draw a breath. They stroked their way nearer and then I saw it was Tada. Ifor was tugging Tada along, holding his shoulders, while Finn stroked alongside, breathing for Tada, into his mouth. As we hauled him aboard, I saw that he was alive, and I burst into the most ridiculous fit of tears when I saw him. Finn said "Stop that, and get some air into his lungs!", and down he went again for Buck and Peredur, but with no success. And this time, just as he reached us, *Nia Ben Aur* gave up her struggle, and with a great sucking noise, she slithered out of sight.

The raft was getting too small for all of us by this time. Finn, Ifor and Uncle Bob were having to hang on in the sea, which was still very wild. We all looked out for the ship's boat, and for Buck and Peredur, but we had to accept that there was no one left to rescue. We swam around, and managed to collect a few more planks, and some of the rope they were trailing, and lashed them together making quite a bit more room. Ifor and Guto rescued the fire bucket, and a spar from the rigging, but by then it was dark, and too dangerous to venture into the mighty seas that were still heaving us along.

"There's just a chance that they got away in the boat" said Finn. I suspect that he'd seen my grief-twisted face. "We'll spot them perhaps, when the dawn comes up."

Instead, he started checking up on everybody's state of fitness. Tada was still unconscious, but his breathing had grown easier, thanks be to God.

Davy, we had to leave to float away, as there was little enough room for the living, aboard our makeshift raft.

Owen had hurt his left knee and ankle, but Ifor had managed to put his belt round as a makeshift tourniquet. His leg was clearly broken, but as yet we couldn't do anything to help him.

Guto had been bruised in his ribs, but he seemed to be able to breathe steadily, in spite of the pain.

Uncle Bob, Ifor and I insisted that we were O.K.: we had been lucky, all three of us. There was still no sign of Buck, nor of Peredur, and we could see no sign at all of the ship's boat.

We cast about, through the hours of darkness, while the storm still raged. At one point, when the lighting flashed ominously, we all lay down in a heap to present less of a conductor.

As suddenly as it had begun, the storming wind died away. The sun came waveringly over the horizon, and we had a chance to survey our situation. First, we looked hard for any sign of life among the debris that was surfacing around us. There was no sign of human movement as far as we could see, but we were able to recover one or two more planks, to stabilise the raft.

Suddenly I cried out "Tada! Thank goodness, Uncle Bob, he's opening his eyes." And sure enough, his eyelids fluttered open, as if at the sound of my voice. "F'anwylyd bach [*my little darling*]" he whispered, and seeing Owen he stretched out to hold him "Tyrd yma, fy machgen i … [*come closer to me, my boy*]", and he held us both to his heart.

Almost at once, Finn carefully raised Tada, and we found he could sit up. We rigged one of the spars floating near by, to make a mast, and to prop Tada up, and then he was in charge.

From his jacket pocket, he produced an old tobacco tin, in which he always kept a knife, twine, a fishing hook, a compass, and a box of matches.

He reminded us that the most important thing was to keep our eyes peeled for Buck and Peredur, and hopefully, the boat. We had told him by now that Davy was gone, and so he suggested that we sing a hymn, so that we could never forget our friend.

And so we sang once again "Yn y dyfroedd mawr a'r tonnau". I looked about me. Tada looked unbelievably weary, but his voice soared upwards, as it has always done. Owen and Guto were coming to life again, back from that hell of misery. Ifor had his eyes closed: Davy had been his special friend, all their lives. Uncle Bob was a grey wraith, but he sang, and his eyes scanned the waves, as he picked absent-mindedly from the sea, the remains of a crate, drifting past.

All at once, Finn called "What's that?" Every man of us craned to see. He was pointing to a plank, which now and then topped the waves, quite a distance away. We saw nothing, and then, as Tada started to sing, we spied a tiny rag of red material, waving. It took so long to reach even calling distance that the sky was growing really bright. Then Finn slid overboard, and managed to manoeuvre the two floating havens together, and we welcomed Peredur. He had been in the water all night, until he was bumped by his plank of wood, and had scrambled aboard. He was very tired, and very much shaken by his night of lonely misery, when he had thought he would die alone, in the vastness of the ocean. "I heard the Captain singing," he said "At first I thought we were all dead, and in the hereafter, and then I felt sick, and knew I am alive."

"I knew my voice would frighten any devil away", Tada struggled to laugh. "I'd rather have proved it some easier way, just the same!"

"What happened to the boat?", Peredur tried to ask. "No-one has seen any sign, so far," said Ifor, "we're still looking out." I hardly dared to ask whether Peredur had seen Buck, but Uncle Bob asked for me. "No" was the answer. Peredur had seen the boat, but it had been too far off. He thought someone was trying to climb aboard, on the far side, but it had drifted away.

I turned my face away: there was no room to move out of sight, but I couldn't bear to think of them all seeing my tears, and the subject was quickly changed. Tada reached out, and held my hand close.

We saw in the far distance a steam ship, heading across the ocean toward Britain. We all waved and shouted frantically, but with no real hope of being sighted; she seemed to heave to, for ten minutes or so, raising our hopes, but she sailed on immediately, with no sign that she had heard us, and might be looking out for us.

The storm had finally blown itself out by this time, too, and we started to take stock of our situation. We collected another two deals, and secured them crosswise, to strengthen the raft. We paddled madly, too, to reach one of the spars from the rigging, which was drifting past, and so raised a mast. I was delighted to get rid of my petticoat, to rig a sail!

Then, the hardest thing of all. Tada and Bob and Finn had been in a huddle for a while. Owen was lying most of the time in my arms, drifting away occasionally when the raft slid down a wave. Finn inched his way over, and unwrapped my belt from Owen's foot. "We must do something with this leg", he muttered, and ran his fingers down from the thigh. Uncle Bob was beside Tada: I saw them exchange nods, and all at once Uncle Bob eased towards us. At the same moment Finn was busy, his hands running gently down Owen's leg, which had started to swell up. "Tell me when it hurts, Owen," he said. But he didn't need to say so, for as he reached the ankle, Owen's face told the whole story. Once or twice Finn stroked the sore spot, then with the merest flicker of his eyes, he seized the thigh in one hand, the ankle in the other, and tugged the leg bones back into alignment. Bob had grasped both me and Owen in his arms, plainly at an arranged signal, and it was just as well for Owen cried out like a banshee, before passing clean out, and if I could have reached Finn, the torturer, I would have cast him overboard, and hoped for a large whale to swallow him.

I tried to stand up, in my wrath. "You animal ... you ... " I shouted. "Sit down, cariad" Tada cut in. "It is the only way he has any chance at all of keeping the leg. It took a mountain of courage for Finn to try it, even."

"Yes, well, next time, warn me", I muttered, feeling ashamed and yet still furious.

Guto came to the rescue. "Oh, yes, tell your big sister if you want any secret let out of the bag ... ", but he grinned at me, and gave me a chance to deflect my wrath on to him.

Chapter Fourteen

Tada took charge once more, as we drifted. "We must take stock of our situation here, and plan how to reach land again", he said.

"We have no food, no stored water. We have no equipment except the raft, and what was in my mariners tin, in my pocket: the compass, knife, twine, one fishing hook, and the tobacco tin itself. Oh, and the box of matches, though I can't see, just at this moment, how that will help."

He smiled at us as he added "Can I suggest that we all turn out our pockets?"

By the time we had all gone through our pockets, and other secret hidey-holes we had a selection of Swiss pocket knives – some with screw driver tucked inside, which later proved very useful. We had two hankies, one large, one tiny – mine, of course. We had some marbles, three pencils, and not much else. I had a small gold safety pin, a brooch with a sharp fastening pin, a hair slide, and two hair combs.

"Not a lot to get us home," remarked Tada "but we have one another, we have faith, and hope. Water should not be a problem in these storms, but we need to be able to store it, just in case; and we must surely catch some fish, from these shoals all around us." He stopped then.

"Finn", he asked "What do you think should come first?"

"Well now, Captain, my vote is for heading back towards Canada, rather than trying to make it home. I calculate that we are around a hundred miles south and east of Cape Race. There is less danger from submarines, and enemy warships: I don't think they'll hang about this far west. They'll not want to risk sinking American vessels, by mistake, will they! Then, if we can strike the Gulf Stream, the days will be warmer, and the current might carry us inshore."

Tada asked for a vote, and we all agreed it made sense.

"Bob," said Tada, next. "What do you suggest?"

"Well, Capten, I think we should all take off our sea boots – those who are wearing them-, and use them to catch the rain as it falls, and store it. It's not the ideal container, but beggars can't be choosers! It will supplement what we can store in the firebucket." Once again we all agreed.

"Ifor?", Tada asked.

"We should share the watch: two on at all times. Eyes peeled for help."

"Peredur?"

"We'll need to find a way of catching some fish. And I wish we could sing, sometimes. It will make home seem nearer."

"A grand idea," said Tada.

I was quite puzzled, but before I had time to think too much about it, Tada spoke.

"Guto?", and again I was completely taken by surprise. I couldn't believe my ears. Guto grinned at Ifor and said

"Thank God there isn't a lobscouse pot, eh Owen? That Ifor would make a feast of you and me."

And then as he asked "Owen?", Tada smiled conspiratorially at me.

Owen whispered, "I'm dying for a wee!", and Uncle Bob cut in "Anyone using the heads must take into account the direction of the wind!" It made us all laugh, especially Owen.

"And now last, but certainly not least, Rhian?"

I looked around, and I knew what would happen if this lot were left to themselves. I said, "When we catch the fish, and store the water, we share everything out equally. Everybody takes his allotted share." I glared at Uncle Bob and Tada.

"Not leaving more for the young ones!"

Then I frowned equally ferociously at Finn and Ifor, "and no leaving more than their share for the oldies, either!"

"We are all in this together – partners, friends."

They all looked at me stunned into silence. And then they gave me a cheer, surprise, surprise!

And so we set about our tasks. We paired up for the watch: Tada with me, Finn and Owen, Ifor and Guto, Bob and Peredur. Ifor and Guto took the first watch, and Tada asked Uncle Bob to look again at Owen's leg. It was tremendously swollen, and we tore a strip off my rather tattered looking blouse to bandage it.

I was quite relieved then, to see him drifting off to sleep, but Finn noticed.

"Keep him awake, for the moment, if you can, just in case he's injured inside" he said. So that was my task set out for the present.

Guto was quietly getting on with making the raft shipshape, under Finn's watchful eye. Every belt, every twist of string was used, to make sure the few items we had didn't slide away with the rolling of the raft, for the seas were even now quite turbulent.

Uncle Bob and Peredur were taking turn on watch, while the others managed to rig a mast from one of the spars, and fastened to it a flap of sail from the rags of canvas we had rescued from the sea.

When it was just growing dark, and the stars were sprinkling to life in the sky, I felt Tada's hand clasp mine in a frenzy of pain. Then his hand grew lax and cold in mine.

"Uncle Bob", I screamed, and we fought – Uncle Bob, Finn and me – to bring him back to us.

"We must let him go, cariad" said Uncle Bob at last.

"No, no!" I wept, but I knew in my heart he was right.

Uncle Bob took off Tada's trousers and his warm jersey. Owen was sobbing quietly beside me, and I sheltered him in my arms. We said prayers over Tada, and slid his body into the sea.

Behind me voices rang out yet gain, with the words of

> Yn y dyfroedd mawr a'r tonnau,
> Nid oes neb a ddeil fy mhen ...

I closed my eyes, and for a moment wished I, too, was dead. Mam, Buck and now Tada; was I fated to lose everyone I loved to the oceans? As the thought hit me I reached out to hold Owen close. I turned and gazed at him.

"We'll always be together," he said, "you and me, Rhian."

A voice behind us said, "No-one can ever take Nia or your father away from you unless you turn your backs on them. They live always in your hearts unless, you, yourselves, choose to forget."

It was Finn. He was looking up into the sky. "If you wish it, everything you do with your lives will be for them. You are like two little caterpillars on a green cabbage leaf. You are busy just keeping alive and growing: you don't even suspect that some day each of you will change into a chrysalis, and the other caterpillars will think you're gone – dead – for ever. But one day, that chrysalis will break open, and who knows if the beautiful butterfly, fluttering in the sky will look down, and say "That's the cabbage patch, and there are the little wrigglies we left behind. Oh, how wonderfully they are growing up!"

It made Owen laugh for the first time since the storm, and Finn grinned back at him.

"Have you been on a raft before Finn?", asked Guto.

"Yes, and for many days and nights," said Finn, tightness in his voice. "But a little girl spotted my raft, and her mother and father rescued me."

"No, I meant in the middle of the Atlantic Ocean, like this," said Guto.

"I've never been adrift in the *Atlantic* before, Guto" said Finn.

"Look, the Northern Lights", Uncle Bob cut in, and we saw the heavens flickering with sparkling lights like Guy Fawkes night, high above us.

Chapter Fifteen

I found myself slipping away as soon as darkness fell. The days were as much as I could manage.

When Uncle Bob woke me to take the watch with Finn, as Owen was not strong enough yet, I discovered that he had persuaded Ifor to wear Tada's trousers, giving Ifor's own trews to Peredur. This meant I could have Peredur's trousers – the nearest to my size amongst us. Uncle Bob had obviously spotted that I was suffering more from the cold, and from the buffeting of the wind than the men were.

This morning the wind was dying down, but even so it was still very gusty. The sun was dark red on the horizon, glowing like the fire at the steelworks back home in Wales. An ominous sight: red in the morning, sailors' warning, so we were expecting a change sooner or later.

We shared out our ration of water, and then set to, trying to catch a fish with Tada's fishhook. Peredur and Guto were the fishermen for the present, while Ifor was watching the seas for any sign of a ship.

Uncle Bob dressed Owen's leg again, and then he and Peredur took over the watch, so I eased myself under Owen's back, and cuddled him, to keep him warm and safe. I drifted off after a while: not asleep, but in a daydream, and I came to just as Owen whimpered with pain as he turned in waking. Guto was beside him in an instant.

As I eased Owen and myself into a more comfortable position Guto said "How's the leg, then Owen?"

"A bit sore," said Owen.

"Well it's better than a wooden one that you can't feel at all," said Guto – all serious in his looks, and then they both burst into laughter!

"Ew, do you remember Johnny Dot-and-Carry", laughed Guto. "My goodness, he couldn't half land you a clout, with that leg of his though."

"Yeah. Maybe I'll get Uncle Bob to chop mine off so that I can clout all your old pals in Standard Five with it, when we get home." Owen retaliated. Then "Golly, Sis, I'm not half hungry … "

"There you are, then: we can eat leg of Owen," chuckled Guto. "It'll be a bit bony, though."

Once again they both laughed fit to burst, and I thanked the Lord for Guto.

At the moment a shout full of excitement rose "Less chat from you two, and pass over that wooden leg, Owen. We've caught a cod."

Peredur, lying there on the edge of the raft gazing into the depths of the seas in which he had lived a whole night long, thinking he would die there alone and forgotten, had hooked and landed our first food. He hitched it on board, and we all reached out to help him.

"Steady on" called Finn, as the raft rocked perilously.

Uncle Bob speared the fish with his knife; we unhooked the fishhook, which Ifor tucked away safely, I noticed, for our next attempt. The poor fish was staring at us, his eyes wide, until Uncle Bob dispatched him, and then his eyes were like dolls' glass bead eyes. I turned to say "Well done" to Peredur, but I shut up quickly as I saw him staring fixedly, the tears filling his eyes. He blinked, and blew his nose, wiping it on his sleeve, as we no longer had anything as civilised as hankies. I put my hand over his, where he was propped up, twisting away, so as not to see the free running waves whence he had caught his codfish. "All the time in the sea, on his lonesome, and then to get caught by a learner. I feel so sorry for him. Daft, isn't it", he smiled waterily at me.

By now Bob had run his blade down the stomach, and remarked "A young lady, anyway, not a 'him' at all, thankfully", and he scooped out the roe. A precious amount on each outstretched hand, and we were all licking our lips – and then licking our hands, not to lose the tiniest morsel. Then we ate the cod's liver, and it too was delicious. When we got to the flesh I must admit I was not quite so enthralled, but it was food, and our stomachs had been empty for three days and nights. Bob and I stripped the remainder into fillets, and strung them to dry. I noticed Uncle Bob counted the strips, so that the number – twenty one – was divisible by seven; the sign of a born caterer, I teased him.

The inedible bits and pieces were tucked away in a seaboot, to make bait for further attempts. Indeed, Guto settled down to try again, and Owen lay watching him. They saw the ripples made by an enormous fish gliding past but, luckily perhaps, it didn't seem interested in their bait.

"Peredur says we're quite a long way north of the steam ship lanes" said Owen "so we're less likely to be rescued. Is that right, Ifor?"

"Yes, but at least we're not likely to be spotted by submarines, or warships" Ifor replied.

"What we need really," said Uncle Bob, from the mast where he was standing watching the horizon "is something to attract attention when we do sight a ship – any ship! And second, we want some rope, for another fishing line."

We looked around in vain. Every tiny bit of rope that we had managed to salvage, was holding the raft together.

"There's this belt round my leg ... " said Owen, quietly.

"Don't you dare!" the words came loud and clear from Finn. Then he added, joking, "I've used my best skills as a surgeon on that leg ... " We all grinned in relief.

Suddenly I thought, and said quietly to Finn, "If we could get something to cushion the leg: I mean, the bleeding's stopped. Would that help?" Finn looked at me straight in the eyes. "We'll have a check on the leg before the sun goes down. If you can think of anything that would replace the belt, that would be wonderful."

The day passed slowly it seemed, and yet when the sun lit down on the sea, the day seemed to have disappeared in a flash – so little had we achieved.

I sat diplomatically sheltered from sight, using "the heads", and thinking. I unplaited my hair, and combed it out and re-plaited it in two braids, plaited very loosely. Finn was unwrapping the belt and my warm scarf which we had used to bandage Owen's leg. He was kneeling beside Owen but the raft had started to plunge with the waves again, and Ifor and Uncle Bob had to hold him steady, while he eased his hands down Owen's shin towards the dislocated ankle. We were all watching Owen's face anxiously, but he seemed not too uncomfortable.

"It's not so swollen as it was" ventured Ifor.

"No, looks much sounder" Finn agreed. "I think we might ease the belt off – not too much yet, of course."

"Worth a try at any rate" was Bob's observation. "If only we had something gentler to hold it ... "

"Can I borrow the sharp knife, Uncle Bob?" I cut in.

"Afraid I'm going to chop his leg off?" queried Finn. "I'm not, even though Bob's knife is sharp enough."

"Don't be daft" I said "It's for me." Uncle Bob handed over the knife. I reached for my plaits, one at a time, and struggled to cut them off.

"No, Rhian … " They all remonstrated in their own ways. "What on earth do you think you're doing … "

Only Finn said nothing. He took the knife from me, and said "Brilliant, Rhian. Just what we need", as he helped me cut the second braid.

The others were all pussy-struck; Uncle Bob reached out to stop him, but too late. Finn was looking straight at me, face to face, adult to adult. He took the two plaits, and wrapped them firmly but gently, to restrain and as well to cushion Owen's sore leg.

"That's what I call a sister" said Ifor, smiling at me, and suddenly they were all looking at me in happy admiration.

Guto took the belt, and started to wrap it round the mast, where it was locked between two deals. It's strange. I'd have though that Peredur, being more experienced, to say nothing of three years older, would be the one to tackle these sorts of tasks, but Guto is the one who sees possibilities of this kind. On the other hand my admiration for Peredur mounted when he would not let Guto go into the water to secure the belt under the raft. He held his breath, and slid into the rough seas and under the raft to pass the belt back through to the surface, so that it could be secured with the buckle. So we had a mast, at last that was strong enough to risk our tattered home-made sail even when the wind blew stronger.

We unlayed the length of strong hempen rope that had held the timbers on *Nia Ben Aur*, and re-spun it, so that instead of one monstrously strong rope we had three, each one strong enough to hold a codfish. I had run my hand through my hair, which hung like washing on a line round my face, so I no longer needed my hairslides, and gave them to Guto and to Owen to fashion into makeshift fishhooks. Then we had to look for a third hook, but first things first, and we cast the lines the minute we saw a shadow in the sea. Another codfish! It was smaller than the first we had caught, and had no roe, but enough for another set of fillets, hung out to dry.

By this time we had eaten two each of our fillets caught the day before, and I must say that the hanging out to cure them made an enormous difference to the taste: they were absolutely delicious.

The water stored in Tada's and Uncle Bob's old seaboots was "tasty" to put it politely, but as we swallowed our ration we were each and everyone of us glad to have it.

Finn and Ifor decided now, that the mast was firm enough to take a second sail, and we rigged my discarded skirt, which billowed out gaily, in the breeze. It became, of course the source of some ribaldry among my fellow castaways.

"That should bring the matelots in droves", joked Ifor.

"Perhaps we should have kept those chestnut tresses, and flown them at the masthead, above the dress", added Peredur.

It made our situation less depressing, and led on to a really good "Noson Lawen", when we sang songs, and exchanged stories, until only the watchmen were left awake.

Morning came again. Again the sky was aflame, and already the wind was freshening, and the waves were starting to toss our fragile craft about unmercifully. We stowed the extra sail, shared out the remaining stored water, ate the last of our fish fillets, and one way and another each of us was secured to some part of the deals. Peredur was the one who seemed to be suffering most, understandably enough. The two youngsters, Guto and Owen, were still enjoying the adventure of playing Robinson Crusoe. Even the loss of Tada had not really hit Owen yet. That night, in the sea, totally alone had become a nightmare for Peredur from which he could not quite escape. Encouraged by Finn, I sat beside Peredur hoping our companionship would make things easier for him, and I was aghast to realise that sometimes he wasn't certain which was the dream: the nightmare or this.

Rain started to fall, so we were able to restock our boots full of water, but then, water had always been the least of our problems. Next, Ifor, who was in charge of the fishing lines today, announced that we had a whopping great cod on the line, so Uncle Bob and he shared out the roe, and the liver, and stowed the rest away to be dealt with later.

We must have reached one of the strong currents, which run off the Grand Banks – either the Gulf Stream, or more likely, Finn thought, the Labrador Current, good news, if we could survive to enjoy it. The contrary wind, however, growing fiercer by the hour, was making the raft pitch horrifically. We were permanently soaked in salt water, which made the suppurating boils on my skin burn like red hot poker wounds, and I'm sure I wasn't alone in that. Finn had the brilliant idea of making the spare sail, my skirt, into a sort of sea anchor. He used the two strongest fishing lines to tie to the corners of the skirt, which we had already opened up for the sail, and it trailed behind the raft in the water, making our progress a little less like that slide in Blackpool.

Everything we did took so much longer, in this terrifying storm, that the day was gone. As the darkness closed in Uncle Bob and Finn tried to cheer us up with songs again, but I found every song came out as "Eternal Father, strong to save ... " especially when we got to "Oh hear us when we cry to Thee for those in peril on the sea ... "

At this point, I don't believe any one of us, not even Finn, had any notion of exactly where we had been blown. We were all terrified, sad and devoid of all hope of rescue. In vain we took it in turn on watch, to scan the horizon. These hours were hell itself, and I hope I never feel as badly as this again. As the day went on we drank some of our plentiful supply of rainwater, and with some difficulty, Uncle Bob cut the cod up, though mention of hanging it up to dry got peals of very hollow laughter.

Night closed in on us again, but we could barely tell the difference, so black had been this day.

Owen slept, so did Guto. Ifor dozed fitfully, so did Uncle Bob. Finn, Peredur and I slept not a wink.

I was tied to Owen and to the mast; but even so, just the thought of falling asleep terrified me: I must look after him – for Mam as I had promised, and now for Tada too, and for Nain, back home waiting for us in Porthmadog. I knew why Peredur dared not fall asleep, and find himself in the sea, alone once more. As for Finn, he was in charge, in Tada's stead. Could anyone imagine Tada falling asleep when we were relying on him!

The night was so foggy by now that we had no chance of seeing any ships that might pass. By the same token, their crews could not see us, either, and we could have been run down and sunk without trace.

Uncle Bob and Ifor, who had sailed these coasts for ten years or more, thought that might mean we were being driven south and west, towards Sable Island, where the hot and cold currents meet. In the hope that they were right, we scoured the westward horizon, trying to spot the flash of a lighthouse beam, or even the crests of the titanic breakers crashing on to the shifting shallows of the sandy bank.

Nothing appeared through the murk of the grey fog-filled shallows of the sandy bank.

It was difficult to tell when dawn came: there was no break in the gloom until almost mid-day, according to Finn's pocket-watch, and we seemed to drift eastward, only to be driven frantically west by the wayward winds, so it was impossible to decide which way we should try to sail.

We maintained the look-out through these weary hours, but my tummy rebelled at the eternal raw fish diet, and I could face no more. Peredur was quiet and white of face, too.

When Finn's watch showed night was falling, he cajoled us all into singing again, asking Peredur to lead the singing, as the suggestion for a noswaith lawen had come originally from him. That worked to cheer Peredur up, and the rest of us, too, in time, especially as Guto and Owen insisted on actions to the songs.

Eventually, everyone fell into a restless sleep, except for Finn and myself, the watchmen. I couldn't stop shivering. It got icily cold in the dead hours of the night.

Finn wrapped his jacket round both of us, holding me close, so that we both kept warm. I felt almost as if Tada was back, and caring for me.

We didn't wake anyone to take on the watch, as neither of us was sleepy. For the first time I learned that Finn had left his home in the Åland Islands to sail with his father.

"I've never been to Finland, but I've heard of the islands" I said. "I remember Nain telling us about them. I can't remember Finland, though, except in geography lessons at school."

"Your Nain Sarah would call our country Suomi, as we do, I'm sure", he smiled. The hours fled, as he told me about the rocky granite islands, scattered in the sea like stars in the Milky Way.

"Kokar is the island where I grew up. We had a farm, but the land is not good, and the winters are very hard, so our mothers and sisters stay home to farm the land, and we men build sailing ships, to trade around the world, and off we sail in them. Three voyages I had done with my father, on his ship *Sigyn*, and on my fourth voyage, my two younger brothers joined us. They were twins, Eric and Carli, and they had their eleventh birthday the day before we left home."

"Kokar, sounds remarkably like Porthmadog", I laughed.

"Now, perhaps you know why I have always felt so at home there!" he smiled.

"How did it happen that you met Tada, and came to Wales?" I asked.

"We had sailed in *Sigyn*, to Cardiff, and then on with a cargo of coals to Sydney, in Australia. From Australia we set off for Chile, in South America, with a cargo of grain. When we had unloaded in Valparaiso, we went up to Callao, to look for a cargo to take back home." He smiled wryly at me.

"I know I don't have to tell a young lady from Porthmadog the nightmare of facing loading guano, in the Chincha Islands. It is something I can never forget: those wretched Chinese boys and men, wheeling great barrows of horrid smelling birdmuck, until they dropped in their tracks, and were hoyed off the rocks. Not even a decent burial! We had to watch the stuff loaded on board, and then we sailed off southwards, down the coast, to round the Horn."

I could see why he got on so well with our Porthmadog seamen, now. Like us, his island families were close-knit, and cared for other people. I couldn't wait to hear more.

"Just as we were ready to leave, a gang of crimps tried to grab Eric and Carli. They had dodged off to the chandler's to buy a present to take home to Mamma. We got rid of them, Father and me, and got the boys aboard. But they were angry to have lost face, in front of many people in the harbour, and vowed revenge." Finn's eyes were lost in memories, clouded with the pain of remembering. "Two nights later, when we were well off the coast, they boarded the ship, and shot Father and Åke, the mate. They set fire to my little brothers, and I had to watch them die, and then they keelhauled me, and threw me naked, into the sea. I … "

Suddenly we heard a moaning sound from Peredur. He woke, and sat up. He seemed not to know where in the world he was. His face was ghost-like, and he was shivering. Finn wriggled over to help him, and we wrapped Finn's coat round him, this time.

His distress had woken everyone else, so we all drank a little water, and those who could still stomach it ate the last of the fish.

I couldn't face it, then Finn handed me one of the empty seaboots. "Chew on that Rhian" he said.

I looked at him, quite taken aback – shock, worry about his sanity all flashed across my mind.

"Just the chewing action might settle your stomach" he grinned. "You don't actually need to bite chunks off and swallow them."

I was surprised. It seemed to get the juices flowing. Guto and Owen had caught a small fish, again, but I couldn't face it as yet. I might have gnawed one or two bites out of the boots, though!

It was difficult to remember how many days and nights we had been adrift, by now. We were getting colder, more weary, more hungry, and more despondent with every hour that passed.

We sighted another steamship far away on the horizon as darkness fell, but all our singing, shouting and waving was to no avail, – yet again.

Dawn came after another night of despair. The skies lightened to a paler shade of black, as Peredur expressed it, and then were blotted out in a hurricane of snow and ice. We just huddled down in a circle around the mast, hoping that we could keep one another warm.

When the storm abated we were almost too tired to bother. Uncle Bob and the boys had been the official watch, and now Ifor and Peredur took over. Was this the sixth or perhaps the seventh day we had been on the raft?

Suddenly Ifor shouted, "Ship ahoy!" We all scanned the seas around us. In the distance, but moving towards us was a small ship.

We hoisted my old skirt once again, to fly from the mast, and as the ship beat up towards us we stood and waved frantically, and shouted and sang despairingly.

It seemed that she would sail right past us, "Going down north," as Marrion would have said. She was a sailing ship, and as she tacked, we saw a figure at the helm point a finger – in our direction. I can see him, to this day, when I close my eyes.

I found that I was reciting the Lord's Prayer – "Ein Tad, yr hwn wyt yn y nefoedd", and I hardly dared take my eyes off her as the little ship came nearer, for fear she disappeared like a mirage. We could see now that she was a fishing vessel, flying a Canadian flag.

    Of course, it took her quite some hours to beat her way over to us. As she came closer we started to cheer, and to sing again, and to shout. Finn had to warn the lads to keep still: it would have been the last straw to upscuttle the raft when we were so near to rescue.

Chapter Sixteen

Our rescuer was a fishing schooner out of Carbonear. As they drew near enough, they launched one of the little dories from which they fish these waters of the Grand Banks.

They pulled over to us, and took us quickly aboard the schooner.

On board, mugs of coffee were ready and waiting – laced with a teaspoon of rum, I felt sure.

"First things first" was the greeting we got from the master, and the second mug of coffee for each of us was followed with blankets wrapped around us, and a hot butty in each of our rapidly warming hands.

"Slowly now," Finn warned us all. "No need to bolt it down." He grinned at the crew crowding about us, "No one's going to steal it, and you might just make yourselves sick."

The schooner, we learned, was the *Cordelia M.*, fishing out of Carbonear. The master, Captain MacLeod, had two of his sons aboard with him, Hamish and Andrew, and three other young fishermen, and a cook, who was very much Uncle Bob's vintage.

We told them how *Nia Ben Aur* had been blown over in the great storms of the week before; that our Captain and two men were lost. As men who sailed in these most perilous of waters they knew how we must feel, so said little.

"Can you hold out for a few days while we get some fish?", asked Captain MacLeod.

"It's our last chance to fish, for this season. The Ice'll be driftin' down soon, and the fog." He looked at us, rather shame-faced. "It's no' been a good year, what with so many of the young lads wantin' to join the navy, and all."

"Mind, your folks'll not know that you're safe, till we get home."

Finn and Uncle Bob both spoke up together. "We're just lucky that you spotted us, and stopped to rescue us," said Finn, and at the same moment, Uncle Bob was joking, "Ah well, now we'll find out what the ladies spend the insurance money on, and how fast it goes!"

I couldn't help laughing. "How long do you think it'll take for us to pay it back to Lloyds!" I giggled.

All the faces turned to me in amazement. They hadn't realised I wasn't another seaman.

At once Captain MacLeod insisted that I must have an extra blanket, to keep warm. He said I must have his cabin, and he would bunk down with his crew.

"Thank you, Captain," I said "I will sleep in your cabin, if you will promise me that you will use it during the daytime."

"No way, lassie," he gestured fiercely with his clenched fist. "No lady on my boat doesn't have her own place to lay her head, day and night."

"I know how you feel", I insisted in my turn, "but I have been a week as near as dammit, on that pile of deals with my young brother and all these, my friends. I am one of them, and I would like you and your men to be my friends, too."

The Captain's grizzled face split from ear to ear, in a smile. "Spoken like a real seaman's gal" he boomed. "I'll bet your father is a seaman!" he laughed.

He was clearly taken aback by the silence, and looked puzzled.

"My father, mine and Owen's" I told him, "died while we were on the raft.

He was so upset at his unthinking clanger that tears stood in his eyes.

I smiled at him tearful myself. "He would forgive you anything at all," I said. "After all, you are our rescuers.

And so we wrapped up in the warm ganzies and trews shared with us by the lads, and gradually made friends.

There were so many more mouths to feed that Uncle Bob and I got ourselves busy down in the galley, with Ringo, the cook.

As a rule, the dories were manned by two men at a time, but now, with all the extra hands, we managed to stretch the fishing times. Hamish and Ifor paired up, and Drew and Peredur. The two younger lads, Alex and Gil, joined up with Finn. Owen was not fit enough to go in the dories, so he and Guto took on the job of stowing the fish in the salt, down in the hold.

In no time at all, we were learning all about our hosts, and the young ones, in particular knew everything there was to know about Porthmadog, and our families. I felt, as I listened, that we would all be friends for life.

Hamish and Drew were both young and newly married. They both had small children. They confided in me that the extra fish would solve many of their problems through this next winter.

They swore that we had brought them luck, since we were surrounded by shoals of cod and haddock, making the long hours we all spent worth every penny.

Being busy helped me to throw off the misery of losing Tada, and Buck, and also the worry of how Nain would be coping.

At night, while waiting for Captain Mac, as he was known to us by now, to finish in the cabin, I stood on deck, in the bow of the boat. The familiar creaking of the spars, the slap of the canvas and the humming of the ropes made me think about Tada.

I suddenly realised I was not alone. Finn was leaning on the rail, quietly keeping me company. I gazed round at the stars. It was still cold, but with warm clothing and shelter it didn't seem as cruel as the icy storms, which had beset us on the raft. It made the sea our home again, not the enemy it had become for a while.

But even the beauty of the night sky, the brilliance of the stars, could not lift my spirits. I was dreaming of Buck, and of what might have been. Thinking, too, of Marrion and the twins. They would grow up with no father – like Cathy, I thought; like Finn, too, as I remembered his story, which had been interrupted.

Peredur came on deck, and they wandered over to join me. Just then we heard a deep chocolate-coated bass voice roll from below deck. We dashed to listen, and then to join in. From that night, we sang every night until weariness drove us to our berths.

We sang all the old sea shanties, our Welsh songs, and the new world ones: songs about the Grand Banks, and Sable Island and the Tickles from which the fishing boats sail. My favourite of Captain Mac's laments, which he had learned from his father and grandfather, was "Will ye no come back again; Better loved ye canna be … Will ye no come back to me … "

Then one night, he sang the song I'd overheard Tada sing; "The desert were a Paradise, if thou wert there, if thou wert there … " I plucked up my courage to ask him about it. It told him I'd heard Tada sing it, when we first sailed in *Nia Ben Aur*.

"It's Rabbie Burns, who else", he answered. "My father used to sing it to Ma."

They were interested, too, to hear about our 'family' – Marrion and the Twinks, in Rainbow Tickle. We were wondering anxiously whether news of the loss of *Nia Ben Aur* had reached them yet. They would think she had gone with all hands, and I wished with all my heart that Tada, Buck, and Davy too had been rescued, with the rest of us.

Twelve more days we fished, and then, laden to the gunwales, we turned for home. Our luck held: a steady wind blew us in to Carbonear by Thursday night, avoiding a superstitious Friday homecoming. It was three and a half weeks before, that we had left St John's, in *Nia Ben Aur*; four weeks since we waved goodbye to Marrion in Rainbow Tickle. A lifetime.

Arriving in harbour, Captain Mac and Finn went down to the harbour master, to inform the agencies of our rescue.

Hamish and Drew undertook the unloading of the fish, with Ifor and Peredur to help, and as soon as Gil, Alex and Hal spread the word, the whole small town was buzzing around us.

Gil's sister, Anita, arrived with her Sunday-best brocaded dress, and a lovely wide-brimmed hat with a satin ribbon; she insisted that I must borrow them. She had stockings for me, as well, and the fact that her shoes were too small for me was hardly her fault, but she was in tears with disappointment.

When Finn and the Captain came back, we were all assigned to different families, for the next two nights. Uncle Bob, Owen and I stayed with the Captain's wife. She reminded me of Marrion: she was tall and powerfully built, with dark long hair, high cheekbones, and sparkling black eyes. Like Marrion, too, she raised chickens and turkeys, ready for Christmas: she had a garden planted with potatoes, beetroot, turnips, and the empty beanrows and pea sticks were skeletons of what had been collected, dried and stored for winter. A home from home, but it made my heart ache, thinking of Nain, back home in Porthmadog.

Two days later we were on board *Cordelia M.* once more, bound for St. John's.

"The fastest unloading ever", commented Captain Mac. "Don't let the wife talk you into hanging about, mind. If you get wintered here, down North, you won't get out until the spring, when the ice breaks."

Quietly, to me, he added "I know the ladies would love to keep you here the winter long, so that they can spoil you, and match you up with their own lads, but the young one there" nodding at Owen, "he needs to have someone look at that leg. There's the hospital in St. John's, or if we can't get that far there's St. Anthony's."

I asked "Is that Doctor Grenfell's hospital that he set up? That's where Marrion went, when the twins were born, Tada told me. Without Doctor Grenfell and the nurses, they would have died, and probably Marrion, too."

"Ay, that's the one," smiled the Captain. "It's places and people like those that make you proud of the auld country, isn't it." His eyes shone with pride.

So off we sailed, the master, with his sons, Hamish and Drew, Ringo the cook, who had volunteered to keep Uncle Bob entertained; sufficient to sail the boat home again with no further need to fish.

Chapter Seventeen

Being in St. John's again was quite exciting. The first night there we all spent in the hospital; a new experience for me. We were given the all-clear, and allowed to leave, except for Owen, whose leg was quite sore again.

"Just my luck", he complained, after the doctors had splinted his leg, and bound it tightly, forbidding him to walk on it at all.

"Just my luck, indeed" quipped Guto. "To have to stay in this comfortable ward, and be fed three good meals every day, while we live in the seamen's mission, on bread and scrape!" He managed to cheer Owen up, but I was glad the ladies of the seamen's mission couldn't hear him, as the fare they provided was delicious.

It was at the Mission that we first got the wondrous news that Buck, too, had been rescued and my heart leapt in my breast. Suddenly the world was shining with happiness again.

It was one of the ladies who recalled reading of *Nia Ben Aur*, and the terrible sinking. Within hours she had come back with a copy of the Halifax Herald, from Nova Scotia. The report told how *Nia Ben Aur* had been homeward bound, heavily laden with salt fish, and with an extra deck cargo of timber, needed for the war effort. The reporter's journalese style jarred slightly, and I hurried on to read.

As she sailed passed Cape Race, the wind had screwed viciously, and the deals on the deck had made that ship pitch and roll dangerously. Second Officer Llew Bulkeley, it said, had been detailed to take charge of the ship's boat, by Captain Rhys Morris. To stand by to embark the captain's children, who were below deck, and the rest of the crew. Meanwhile Captain Morris would cut loose the timbers.

"Too late!" wrote the reporter. A twisting spiral of wind caught her, and the ship turned over, and disappeared, with an enormous sucking noise.

Llew Bulkeley searched the waters for any sign of survivors, in vain. All that resurfaced were a few of the "satanic deals which had sunk the gallant sailing ship", so the pressman pontificated.

By this time night was falling, and when H.M.S Sea Warrior

appeared on the horizon, Second Officer Bulkeley fired two flares, and was taken aboard.

As there was no sign of any wreckage, Captain Ashfield, of the 'Sea Warrior' felt sure that the little boat must have drifted away from the scene of the sinking, and persuaded Mr. Bulkeley that the time had come to abandon hope, and sail with them for home.

Captain Rhys Morris, the story went on, had recently married a Canadian bride, and was the father of twin daughters, who would now grow up in Labrador, without him; and his daughter Rhian and son Owen had perished with their beloved father.

Reading the newspaper report reminded us all of the horror and grief which Marrion, and all our families in Porthmadog must have been feeling, all these weeks. Uncle Bob's family, Nain, Morfudd and her little ones, Peredur's father and mother, and Guto's Mam, too. Our friends, as well: Rhiannon and Jenny, Griff, Mrs. Morgan, so many who would have wondered what had happened.

Looking after Owen, and getting back to Porthmadog took on a new urgency and excitement, and knowing that Buck was safe gave a new glow to life, for me at any rate.

After three or four days, Ifor and Peredur had been found berths on a ship heading for home, which was short handed. I had noticed on the way down from Carbonear that Peredur still looked haunted when he watched the waves stretching empty, out to the horizon. Ifor, too, was not looking forward to facing Morfudd, his wife, with the details of Davy's death. We missed them terribly.

The days seemed interminable until Owen was given a time when he could leave the hospital, and then Uncle Bob got a job as cook, on a U.S. steam ship, heading for Liverpool. They agreed to take Guto, too, as his apprentice, and he managed to get Owen and me booked to travel home on the liner, as passengers.

"What will you do, Finn?" Guto asked.

"I'll get away down to Buenos Aires, to see if I'm in time for the 'Endurance', I think," Finn smiled at us. "There's a Swedish boat sailing for Buenos Aires on Saturday, and if I'm too late to catch them there, she's going on to South Georgia, to the whaling station, and I'm pretty sure to be there before Captain Shackleton leaves for the Weddell Sea.

Couldn't be better, from my point of view."

"I suppose there wouldn't be room for an apprentice?" Guto asked shyly.

"Next time, maybe", Finn smiled at him.

"Two apprentices?" queried Owen. Finn grinned encouragingly at him.

Next day we went down to the quay, and waved Finn off.

It was heartbreaking to wave goodbye, not knowing when we would see him again. He had taken Tada's place for Owen and for me, as far as possible: making decisions, dealing with the port authorities, even helping us out with his own money, when necessary. I had insisted that he must keep records of all the money he had spent to help us, so that I could give it to Mrs. Morgan, to keep till he got back.

We hoped he'd catch up with the 'Endurance'. It was obvious that he longed to be with the intrepid explorers.

Waving goodbye was made easier for me. My heart was set on getting back to Porthmadog, to see Buck again. I could have danced all the way there over the ocean, without even feeling tired, now that I knew he had been rescued.

So we travelled across – the first time I had ever been on a steamer.

It had none of the excitement or beauty of a sailing ship, but once our story was known, everybody made a great fuss of us – which Owen and Guto revelled in.

I must admit, I enjoyed being the centre of attention, too. I still had Anita's pretty dress, and I had bought some more dresses in St. John's having nothing of my own to wear.

It was interesting to see how different was life aboard a steam ship, but some of this would be due to my being a passenger, for the first time, with no allegiance to the master or to the owners. Some would be due to the size of the ship, too, no doubt. Small tramp steamers, touting for cargo, would be more like our little sailing ships.

Once again Guto and Owen made friends at once. No rigging to climb this time – it was forbidden territory to mere passengers – but they soon joined the card-school, and the betting syndicate, putting their money now, in wartime, on whether we would sight a U-boat!

All the young seamen were envious of their adventures, so they were in great demand.

The engine-room, of course, was a totally new field for exploration, and they soon had friends eager to explain the intricacies and the advantages, too, of turbine driven ships.

Uncle Bob kept me company when he could, but it was not long before I found that the initial interest of the few ladies on board was rapidly doused by their nervous fear that such a fate might happen to them and their families – a possibility they refused to dwell on.

I was lucky enough to discover the store of books provided for the entertainment of passengers, even in wartime, and so I was usually to be found ensconced in a sheltered corner of the main forward deck or hiding from the rain in a similar hide-away in the saloon.

I read the books of the Bronte sisters, Jane Austen, John Buchan, and the days passed in a dream world.

One day I really struck lucky. I was looking through the volumes for something new to read, when Captain Miles came in.

"Changing books again!" he teased. "You really are a book-worm, aren't you"

I said, "You don't have many exciting adventure stories. It's rather disappointing."

"Ah, well now," he answered, "I think I can trust you to respect my little secret," and he opened a cupboard, hidden away behind the table. It was full of real adventure books.

"This is where I keep the key" he showed me his hidey-hole. I chose Jack London's 'Sea Wolf', for a start, and for the rest of the voyage I was able to bury myself in the books of Somerset Maugham, Robert Louis Stevenson, Joseph Conrad, and others.

"Sometimes the ladies are unkind enough to begrudge me my reading. They want me to socialize with them in the saloon, and to that end, they have been known to 'borrow' all my favourite authors!", he explained, rather shamefaced.

I couldn't help giggling, and yet even in these two or three days I had noticed how some of the younger ladies surrounded him, the minute he made an appearance in the saloon.

Nights were better. I watched the stars appear, and the moon climb the skies, until, sooner than I had dared hope, we were approaching the Irish coast, and then within days, sailing past Holyhead, and Sir Fôn and along our Welsh coast.

At last we sailed into Liverpool. It was February by now, and the Liver birds were blanked out by pouring rain, black with city soot and smoke.

I looked hopefully for someone meeting us. In vain.

When we went to Customs House, though, there were messages from Nain and from Guto's mother, saying that as they weren't able to get information about when we would land they would wait in Porthmadog, till they heard from us.

I was ready to burst into tears, when from the open doorway we saw hands waving, and a cheerful Welsh voice shouting "Croeso'n ôl Tada. [*welcome home Daddy*]"

It was Uncle Bob's daughter, Lowri, with three little ones crammed into an enormous black pram, and what a fuss she and all her friends made of us.

First she enquired about the times of the trains for next day, and then she took us home to Bootle, where there were so many Welsh seamen, and schoolteachers, that one of her friends joked with us, "What's the capital of Wales?"

"Bootle", came the answer from a dozen voices!

While Lowri and I made up beds for the four of us, Bob and the boys took the three little ones down to the local sweetie shop, carried triumphantly on their shoulders.

When they returned, they had chocolates for Lowri, wee Willy Woodbines for her husband, and I overheard the oldest of the children, Blodwen, say to her Mam "Grandpa said we could have one each of everything on the sweetie counter, Mam", and they were laden with sherbert fountains, bulls' eyes, lollipops, sherbert dabs – everything imaginable.

He had left money with Mr. Jones, the shop, for a repeat, in time for Easter – but the children didn't know that yet. I gathered that normally, their sweetie money was a halfpenny every Saturday, for which the older two girls helped their mam tidy their attic bedroom.

No wonder Grandpa Bob was popular!

Chapter Eighteen

Next day we were at the station for the first train which would take us home.

Through the Mersey tunnel, where Guto and Owen made ghostly noises, though their chances of frightening our fellow passengers were nil. Most of them were soldiers, on their way south, to the training camps, or back to the trenches.

A lady seated beside Uncle Bob remarked that it was sad to see how young most of them were, but to seafarers, of course, this was the age at which young boys normally left home to sail the world.

We had to go right down as far as Gobowen, where we changed trains, at the junction, and went away through the mountains for home. Tears stood in my eyes, as we finally passed Llyn-y-Bala, and then across the estuary to Porthmadog.

I noticed that Uncle Bob had one or two surreptitious blows of his nose, too. The two boys were unimpressed!

We pulled into the station at Porthmadog. Not a soul to welcome us, I could feel my heart freezing in dismay. What was wrong? Was Nain ill?

Suddenly, a voice rose into the air, a spirit voice, for there was no-one to be seen.

"Mae hen wlad fy nhadau yn annwyl i mi ... [*the land of my fathers is dear to my heart*]"

I knew that voice!

When she had seen us off at Lime Street station, in Liverpool, Lowri had gone straight down to the post office, and sent a telegram to her mother, Uncle Bob's Milly, to tell them that we would be on the train, and so we were welcomed home by Rhiannon and all our friends, who had mitched out of afternoon school, to show how thrilled they were to have us back.

Owen jumped off the train, almost before it stopped at the platform, and into Nain's arms. I must admit, I wasn't more than a whisker behind him. Guto, too, ran to his Mam for a hug and a load of kisses, until he realised his mates were watching; Uncle Bob was left to collect our gear, and get it off the train before it puffed away. But then we all made room for him to hold tight to Milly, his wife, and to hold her close. The tears mingled on his face and on hers.

Never one to miss out on a chance to tease, Uncle Bob grinned, "See how sorry she is to see me back. It's goodbye to that fancy lodger now!" Milly pretended to smack him.

"Doesn't change, does he!", she smiled at us all.

Rhiannon and the crowd sang all the way to Guto's home in New Street, and then to Uncle Bob's, and then we were off to Chapel Street.

Auntie Good-Girl, who was with Nain, explained that Nain had been ill, and rather than leave her on her own they had brought her from the hospital, to stay across the road with them. She hoped we wouldn't mind staying there too, for the present.

Now that I had time to look, Nain did look very frail, but with the old indomitable spirit, she had prepared a feast fit for warriors; all our favourite dishes at one sitting.

Even in the joy of being home, though, my heart flashed to thoughts of Buck, and I wondered how long before I'd see him.

Rhiannon and Jenny arrived early the next day.

"Back to school, mind", they said – like a comic double act.

And so it went. In no time at all we were back at our school desks – Owen and me, – and Guto, too, at the head master's suggestion, came back while he waited for a berth on another ship.

No word came from Buck.

We knew that he had heard of our rescue, and our arrival in Porthmadog, for Cathy had written a lovely letter.

She told us how much Buck had helped her, when she had to talk to the Lloyds Insurers, on Marrion and the Twinks' behalf, and how glad she was to hear we were rescued.

She was eager for us to take over the negotiations, so that she could get home, to help Marrion with the farm.

Not a word, still, from Buck.

That was when my world shattered to smithereens, for Cathy's next letter went on to say that she and Buck had married just a few days before the news came that we had been rescued. She felt so sad that they hadn't known, or they would have waited, so that we could all come to the wedding.

After his short time on the Sea Warrior, when he was picked up, Buck had decided to join the Royal Navy, for the war-time, rather than go back to the merchant service. They had married when he heard that he was to sail forthwith.

For a moment I wished I had gone down, with Tada, and then I shook myself in anger and at the same time in despair.

"What about Owen?" I said to myself. "What about Nain?" It was up to me now, to look after them.

Two days later, Cathy and Buck arrived. They moved straight into 5 Chapel Street, without even calling on us, to ask for Nain's permission to stay there. I found it rather strange, even rude, and it didn't chime at all with the Cathy I thought I had known in Newfoundland.

As it happened, I overheard a muttered discussion between William Lloyd and Auntie Good-girl.

"It's not good enough", I heard him say. "They can't just move into Sarah's house like that, without so much as a 'by-your-leave'! You persuaded me not to intervene when he came here before, but to turn up now, to walk in as if he owned the house, especially now Rhian and Owen are home, is pushing his luck too far."

Before he could say anything more, Auntie Good-girl cut in, her voice sharp with pleading,

"Well, don't you dare say a word, William. All you'll do will be to drive Sarah and the children out of this house, and I won't have that! Just hold your horses for now, please, please, Will."

William Lloyd smiled wryly. "I know. I'm not going to do anything about it for the moment. It's just that I'm puzzled. I'm sure the Canadian lassie knows nothing about what is going on, in her mother's name, any more than Marrion herself does. Still, I'll hold my tongue if you insist, until Sarah and the young ones are ready to go home."

By now, it was time for school, so I had no chance to find out more, and things stayed as they were.

I was learning how cruel life can be. Buck never once spoke to me, except in company, and he and Cathy behaved like any love besotted newly weds. I had been forgotten – perhaps buried was the word I wanted.

A week later they came to say goodbye. Buck had been told to join his ship. He was sailing later that week, in H.M.S. Sea Warrior, and Cathy was sailing home on a steam ship, leaving from Bristol.

Next day, Nain decided that she felt well enough to move back into her home, with Owen and me to keep her company. William Lloyd insisted on going first, and out of curiosity, I followed him, on the pretext of carrying Nain's comfortable easy chair.

I noticed that Nain's keys were not used to open the door: Hugh Owen, the blacksmith's man was there, forcing what were clearly new locks.

Mr. Lloyd caught me watching.

"Not a word, mind, Rhian annwyl", he whispered. "Your Nain would be so upset, if she learnt what has been going on. Just as well it will be put right before she or Marrion find out."

For myself, I was totally bewildered, and when the locks had been opened, and new ones fitted, I was angry, too, and at the same time, so sad.

Many of the personal things from Nain's bedroom had been taken across to Auntie Good-girl's house, of course, when Nain was ill, but her room had been turned into a bare guest room. Then when I saw Tada's bedroom I was even more devastated. Nain had always kept it as if he might walk into it that very night. The fact that he might be in Sydney, in Newfoundland, or even in San Francisco didn't matter, it was his room. Now, the bedroom was made up, clearly, for Mr. and Mrs. Llew Bulkeley. Tada was wiped away, as if he had never existed – nothing of him left at all.

I went up the rickety old stairway to the attic bedroom which Nain had divided for Owen and me. There stored roof high, were boxes, old curtains draped over piles of books, clothes, a whole lifetime of paraphernalia. The worst thing was, I could hear, in my mind, Buck's voice, disparagingly writing off my whole life, everything and everyone I had ever loved.

Chapter Nineteen

The next months fell back into the usual routine. Rhiannon was working hard at her singing lessons, Jenny and I had been offered a place at Bangor Normal Teachers' Training College, provided we passed our Highers examination.

Peredur had been home, and he and Jenny were clingingly in love. Rhiannon was able to meet her poet now and again, though I heard rumours that she was not his only love. Time would tell.

I was the odd man out. Buck's cruelty had soured me against the whole idea of love. I had become a real cynic.

I became lost in misery: this was worse than losing Buck to the Atlantic. My life became a grey wilderness. Rhiannon and Jenny tried so hard to help me, and I knew that for Nain, and Owen's sakes, I had to pull myself together. But it was not the old me. I felt older, wiser in the ways of the world, expecting nothing – a grey wraith, although hiding my disillusion as well as I could.

I joined in everything at school; was the life and soul at all the parties, because nothing mattered all that much, any more. It was true that gradually, I found myself wakening to life again, but underneath, there remained this great hole of misery and scepticism.

One day, Buck arrived back in Porthmadog. His time at sea with the Royal Navy had been very short, and now he was stationed in safety and comfort at a Shore Establishment, while all our other friends sailed the perilous seas, or fought in the trenches.

"I wonder whose wife wangled him that cushy hidey-hole?" I said scathingly to Jenny.

Nain had received the insurance payment for her three sixtyfourths of *Nia Ben Aur*, but William Lloyd had still not been able to recover anything for Owen and me. Of course, settlement had been started on the assumption that Tada, Owen and I had gone down with the ship, which Buck's lawyers, acting still, they claimed, on behalf of Marrion and the twins, used as an excuse for the delay.

At Christmas, we all got lovely presents in the post, from Marrion. Mine was a picture of two little boys, warming themselves at the fire. It was a print, of course, of a painting by one of the Group of Seven Canadian artists, and I hid it away ready for when I hoped to be in Bangor.

Owen's present was a kit, to build a model aeroplane, and he was absolutely thrilled with it. He and Guto, and his old classmate Griff, set to, to build it, and then to fly it on the Traeth Mawr, full of their own importance, because the other boys only had kites to fly.

"Do you remember when that Mr. Harmel came from Germany and flew from the Traeth, in his aeroplane?" I heard Robyn Meredith ask them. "At the National show it was." I don't think any of us realised that the same German planes would be strafing our own menfolk, in the trenches in France.

In just the little time we had been together, Marrion seemed to have got so close to us – perhaps it was because Tada had talked of us, before we met.

Nain and Mrs Morgan had had letters from Finn. He had missed the "Endurance" at Buenos Aires, and again at South Georgia. Fortunately, Captain Shackleton hadn't to sail shorthanded, as he had recruited a young ship's officer who had been left without a berth, in Buenos Aires. In the meantime, Finn had taken a berth as Mate of the little steamship which ferried coal for the steam ships to South Georgia, from Chile.

"I bet he hopes to find a way of joining the expedition, or helping them some way or other, sooner or later," said Guto.

"Lucky dab!", was Owen's comment.

With so little to side-track my attention, my exam results in August were good, and in September of 1916 Jenny and I went off to Bangor to College, just after my seventeenth birthday. We missed Rhiannon a lot. She had gone down to London to the Royal College, with the help of a special scholarship from Mrs. Casson.

Who should be on the train when we saw her off, but Elsyn, who had joined the army. They were already spouting poetry and songs at one another long before the train pulled out of the station, and then at the last moment, we saw the two of them locked together, hanging out of the window and waving frantically at us all. In the distance, soaring to the heavens, we heard "Ffarwel i ti Gymru, ffarwel i'th fynyddoedd [*Farewell to you, Wales, farewell to your mountains*]," and then they were gone.

Owen was missing Guto, too. When school ended he had gone to Tyneside for training in the use of steam turbine engines.

"Well, that was on the cards ever since we sailed home on the 'Alexander'," was Uncle Bob's reaction. "Parsons yard, in Jarrow he's gone to has he. Well no better place to learn about turbines." While Guto was away, Owen renewed his friendship with Griff, Jenny's little brother, who was in the same class at school.

It was in November that we heard that Grandma De Winton had died. She wished to be buried in the churchyard in her own old home, at Maeshyfryd, and I felt that we should go to the funeral, in spite of her indifference to our existence, over these last years. William Lloyd brought Nain, Owen and Auntie Good-girl to Bangor, driving his new Ford motor-car. I joined them, and off we went along the coast, to be greeted with looks of disbelief from many of the mourners at the church.

Afterwards we returned to Maeshyfryd, which still roused sad memories in my heart. I thought Owen had forgotten, but suddenly, as we drove up to the gates, he shivered.

"That's the lodge, isn't it? Where 'Banger' James lived, I bet I could make him pay now for all the sly beatings he gave me!", he muttered. 'Banger' James was the gardener's son, nearer my age than Owen's, and I had not realised then that he was making my little brother's life such a misery.

We all went in to the house, where a reception was laid out in Grandma's elegant drawing room. The family seemed to have flocked from all parts of the kingdom, and were invited to stay for a formal reading of her will.

William Lloyd ushered us to the study door, and was greeted with raised eyebrows. He explained that, as Nia's offspring, and therefore Mrs. De Winton's grandchildren, we were interested parties. This was greeted with shocked silence, but the solicitor, Mr. Parry stood aside for us to go in.

Grandma de Winton did not so much as mention our existence in her last will and testament. All went to her more recently acquired friends and family.

Mr. Parry looked at us and at William Lloyd, clearly in some trepidation.

"If you wish to challenge the will … " he began.

"We're not interested ... " I cut in.

"If she had left me her money, I'd be bequeathing it to a home for stray dogs." Owen said, in a surprisingly loud and adult voice.

Mr. Parry frowned as he looked at William Lloyd, who remarked that when Nia had died in childbirth, her personal effects had been brought here, to her old home, where she had been buried, and these personal belongings – her wedding ring, her jewellery, and the sea-box in which they had been brought here, surely were now the property of her only two children

Also, he pointed out to Mr. Parry, that on Grandma De Winton's say-so, Llew Bulkeley was handling our father's estate, including the Lloyds' Insurance settlement on *Nia Ben Aur*, and of that, nothing at all had yet accrued to his children, namely Owen and me. He stressed that in fact neither Grandma nor any of the De Winton family were entitled to so much as a farthing of Tada's insurance, once we two had been rescued from the raft. On our behalf, William Lloyd and Nain as our guardians demanded a statement of the accounts from Mr. Parry's firm, as they had acted for Grandma and Mr. Bulkeley.

Consternation reigned.

We went outside and Nain sank into her seat. She struggled to hold back the tears.

"Nain, you didn't want us to take their filthy money," came from Owen.

"No, no, my boy. Tears of pride these are, pride in both of you," and she smiled a watery smile.

We both hugged her tight, while Auntie Good-girl and William Lloyd looked on approvingly.

Mr. Parry, the solicitor, came to us then, and promised that Nia's sea-chest, and her other effects would be ready for us to collect that evening, and on that note we left.

Later that night, I went with William Lloyd back to Maeshyfryd, and over to the store-room where, under eagle-eyed supervision we sorted out Nia's sea-box, and the few things of hers that we could find – some picture albums in particular, and off we returned to Bangor, where Jenny was waiting anxiously, as it had grown so late.

I hugged Nain, Owen, Auntie Good-girl, and even stretched up shyly to kiss William Lloyd.

"I know you'll look after Nain and Owen, for me, while I'm away; and thank you for everything you've done for us."

He smiled his sad smile, and kissed my forehead, and they left.

Chapter Twenty

One more week and term finished for the Christmas holidays. Home we went, Jenny and me, like fledgling homing pigeons, drawn back to the nest.

We came into the station, wondering who would be waiting to welcome us back. Anxiously we scanned the platform, and then we spotted Owen bouncing up and down and waving madly. Jenny's mam was with him, and who could that be, beside them? It was Finn. It was almost a year and a half since he had waved us off, as we sailed from Canada in the "Alexandra". He had arrived home in Porthmadog just the day before, and had come to meet us, bringing a borrowed pony and trap so that Nain could come too. Home then, to Chapel Street, where Auntie Good-girl was waiting with a real welcome home tea, preceded by hugs and kisses all round.

Jenny's father came later, and took them home, and then we settled down to exchange news.

We already knew that Finn had not been able to reach the "Endurance", and so he had taken a post in "Louisa", the steam ship that ferried coal from Chile to South Georgia, and now we heard that he had been very glad that he had been able to stay on in the islands. "Endurance" had been beset by the pack-ice, and during the southern winter she had been crushed, so that the men of the expedition had taken to their three small boats, and had landed up on Elephant Island. Captain Shackleton had decided that they must find help, and with five of the men, he had set out for South Georgia. They had landed in King Haakon's Bay, on the uninhabited side of the island, then realising that they could sail no further, Shackleton and two of the men had climbed over the mountains, and descended to the whaling station, to seek help.

By this time it was almost midnight, and Finn promised that he would finish the story next day, after school.

We waved goodnight to him, and then Owen went through his nightly ritual of locking all the doors, while I helped Nain settle into her bed, and made sure her bedside lamp was out, and then I kissed her goodnight.

I looked in on Owen, in Tada's old room, to find that he had set out his school gear ready for the morning, and then fallen, exhausted, fast asleep, with only his boots and trousers removed. I tucked the blankets around him, and kissed him gently, so as not to wake him.

All this done, I climbed wearily up the creaking old steps to my attic bedroom. It was plain and barely furnished by De Winton standards, I knew, and even in comparison with my room at College, but I had spent such happy years here, with Nain.

Carefully, I made a space for my lamp, and looked about, contentedly. My pictures were still on the wall around my bed. Pasted on the ceiling above my head, where I could lie in bed and see it constantly, was a map of the world, from an old seaman's atlas, all the trade routes marked clearly. I had always loved to trace where Tada's ship, *Olwen* might be, on their voyages around the globe.

I sat down, eased myself achingly out of my heavy woollen dress, and my stays, pulled on my warm winceyette nightie, and brushed my hair until it shone.

And then my eyes fell on the wooden chest, tucked in below the slope of the roof.

What was this? Suddenly I realised: it was Mam's sea-box that we had collected from Maeshyfryd.

Like a shot, I was out of bed again, wrapped myself in my blanket, and reached for the lid. The key was in the lock. I opened the chest, and found a beautiful painting of Traeth Mawr, on the underside.

Suddenly my mouth was dry. What should I find? Nia, my mother, for whom I had promised to look after her baby son – well I'd done that! If only I could remember Nia herself. The carving on the stem-head when Tada unveiled his new ship had brought her back to life for me, like a light turned on in the darkness, but these following years of upheaval had dimmed her picture from my memory again.

I gritted my teeth, and I unwrapped a mysterious parcel at the top of the box. Toys! Beautifully made, but still toys. I was intrigued when I examined them more carefully: they all seemed to be antipodean, from the other side of the world. They must have been well played with, especially a kangaroo, with a baby-joey, I think they call them in Australia – in her pouch.

I wrapped them up, again. When, if ever, this war was over, and we saw Marrion and the Twinks again, they might like to play with them, I thought.

Underneath, I found some song books, some hymn books, and then a leather covered book, with a glorious portrait of a lady, looking eagerly forward, her flowing golden hair drifting behind, as if a light breeze was stirring it.

I opened it. A diary. It must be Mam's, Nia's.

Curling myself up, to get the best of my oil-lamp's glow, I began to read.

Nia's Diary

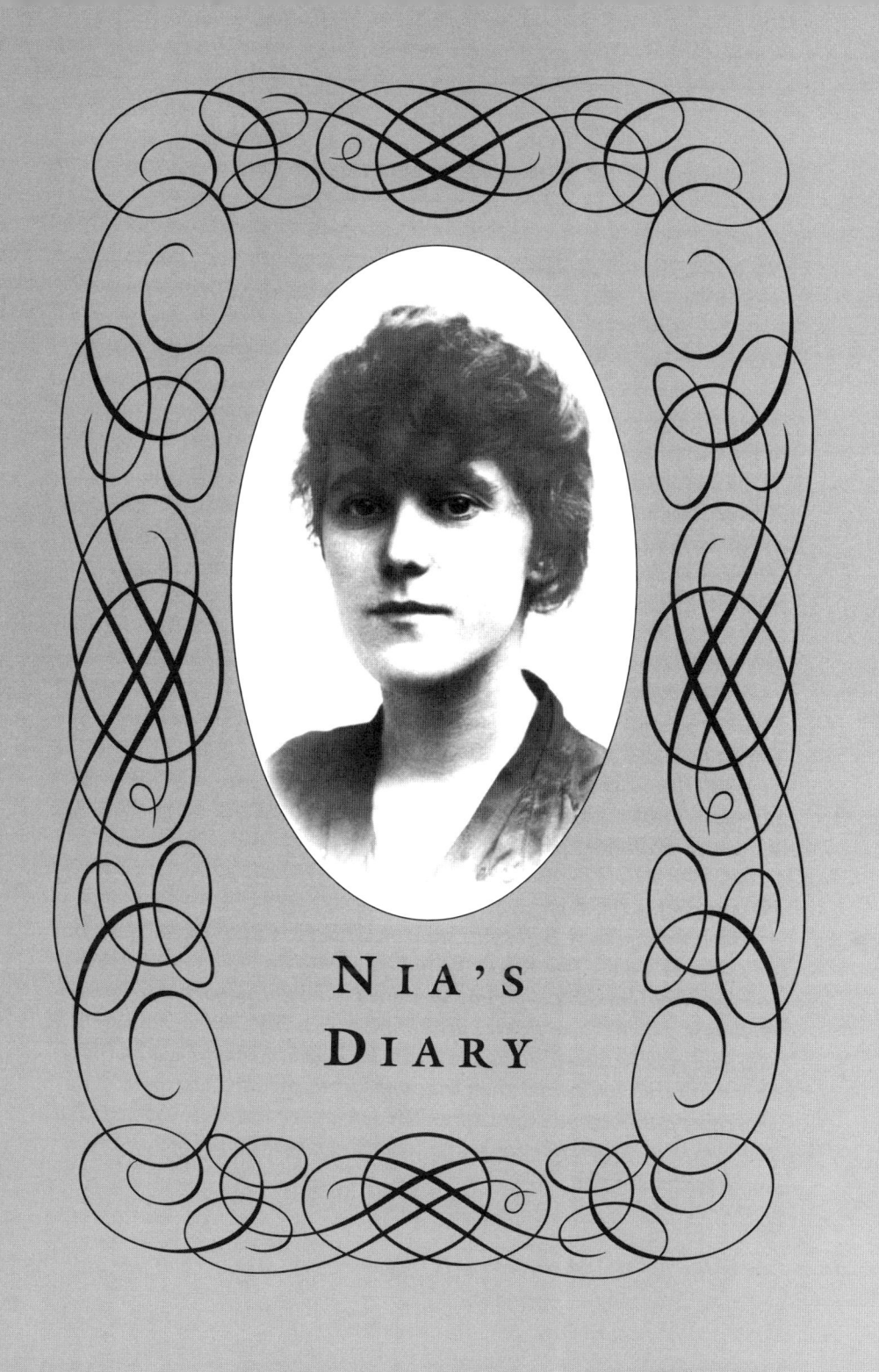

The voyage of 'Olwen', November 1905
Diary of Nia Morris, for my daughter Rhian

I have decided to write down the story of this voyage for you, Rhian.

It is quite likely that this will be the last time we sail with Tada, in Olwen, for some years. The time has come, my darling Rhian, for you to go more regularly to school.

I have loved teaching you reading, writing and some elementary arithmetic, but that is not enough. It is time you made friends among the girls of your age, in Porthmadog, – and the boys, too, of course.

We shall always have this diary to remind us of happy days, when 'Olwen' sails without us.

November 10th 1905

We left Porthmadog today on the tide. We are loaded with slates for Hamburg, and so we are also loaded with presents for Rosa and the family, and our friends over there.

Lewis Jones in the Wave of Life towed us out over the bar in surprisingly pleasant weather for the time of year. It will be good to see Rosa and Walter again.

November 21st 1905

What fun we have had since we arrived here in Hamburg. Yesterday was Walter's daughter Anja's birthday, and Rosa, her 'Oma' Rosa, as she calls her Grandmother, had arranged a delightful party for her. She is almost a year older than you, Rhian; this is her sixth birthday, and you will not be seven years old until July, next year, of course. How those children must miss their mamma, since she died last year.

Today has been most exciting. The fair weather which has lasted all the way here, and while we unloaded, suddenly disappeared and heavy snow fell overnight.

You obviously enjoy snow sports, Rhian. Out came the sledges for you younger ones, while the older boys and girls raced along on their skis higher up the slopes. This is when it is an advantage to be on the hills, above the city.

You all joined together to build your friend the snowman, – no, create is the word, not build! And finally we had a wonderful picnic beside the enormous bonfire. Steaks and sausages, potatoes cooked in the embers, and lots of chocolate torte to finish.

Rosa had brought some of the children down to wave goodbye from the quayside, and she hopes to see us again before too long. She has been quite upset to realise that this is the last full voyage with 'Olwen' for you and me, but she does understand. I promised that we would come during the school holidays, whenever possible, just for a few days, and all the young ones are sure they will see us in Porthmadog, as soon as we get back from this trip. Henk and Anja and Bernice came to wave goodbye, do you remember?

The wonderful thing about the life of a voyager is that you know you will see your friends and family again, with new stories to tell, and new friends to share all over the world.

It's not goodbye, but "Haste ye back", that they wave to us. It's not goodbye we wave to them, either, but "Till we meet again".

As I read these entries in Mam's diary, I couldn't help comparing everything that happened then, with our last visit to Hamburg, in *Nia Ben Aur*, as well as with the present day.

Now, there were no sailing ships taking slates to Hamburg. Our friends, the Elkans, the Petersens and the other shipping agents had risked their lives, and those of their families to get us out of danger.

Their families and friends were now "the enemy", as we must be to them, in the eyes of the authority.

Just as we heard with sadness of ships and crews like the 'George Casson' disappearing without trace, so they would know of ships and merchant seamen who had disappeared on the high seas, or in British ports when war was declared, and who had not been heard from since.

War has a lot to answer for.

And there in my bed in Nain's attic I prayed for the safety of Henk and Vincent, Anja and Bernice, and the rest, along with our own young people.

Then I became engrossed again in Mam's story.

December 5th 1905

Today we left the West India Dock, in London, where we had loaded a general cargo for Sydney, New South Wales, – half a world away.

We were towed out in fairish weather, passing Captain Scott's ship, Discovery, *on the way.*

As soon as I have sat down to write today's story in my diary, the boat has begun to toss in heavy seas, so I must beg forgiveness from whoever reads my diary, for the untidiness of this scrawl.

Never mind, too fair a start to a voyage always makes me wonder what may lie in wait.

December 17th 1905

We are having diabolical weather. My digestive system has gone on strike. Several of the crew are sea-sick when they get up, and even worse when they return to their berths. Fortunately, Rhys, Bob, and young Ifor, and his friend, Davy, the boy who is on his first voyage, are fine. I must not forget to mention you Rhian seem not even to notice that the ship is playing at rivalling Blackpool's Big Dipper.

What was that nonsense I wrote about too fair a start!

December 20th 1905

The weather has not improved. I am trying to prepare for Christmas Day, but not with any great enthusiasm.

The Christmas presents are wrapped, ready for Santa to put under the tree, which we are having difficulty in continuing to hide from Little Miss Nosey Parker.

Another drawback is that several of the young ones could do with the warm dry woollies I have made for them. By Christmas day we'll be further South and the sun will probably come out, and they'll be stowed away till next year!

Christmas Eve, December 24th 1905

All is ready. Rhys had helped me to retrieve the tree from the hold, and it has been suitably adorned.

As soon as he had returned to the deck, to check the watch, Bob and the men helped me to uncover Rhys's present. It's still a secret, though.

This trip has been a nightmare. The wind has howled like a thousand banshees all day and night long.

Given normal weather, we should be approaching Madeira Island, but we are only now rounding Cape Finistere.

Christmas Day, December 25th 1905

Rhian has had a wonderful Christmas day. Santa had left her some sweeties by her bedside, and a sketch-pad and crayons, to keep her busy.

I had made a little suit, like a pair of strong warm winceyette pyjamas, so that she can climb about on deck. She is always trying to keep up with the lads of the crew. She can wear her skirt over the top, when we are in port.

I'm afraid the pyjama suit was not to our young lady's liking at first. She stamped her feet, refusing to look at girls' pyjamas, and wanting trews, like the boys, until Davy called it a monkey suit, and wished he'd had one, when he ran away to the circus, once.

Nanna Rosa, from Hamburg, had made a pretty dress for her, and I had made a tiara for her hair, to match.

The tree was hung with toy animals, a surprise even to me. And then I realised they were presents for you, Rhian, from the lads, and they were all Australian animals: a kangaroo, with her baby in her pouch, a wallaby, a koala bear, and a crocodile, with enormous teeth. They must have kept them hidden away.

They all appeared for Christmas dinner, wearing their sweaters that I had knitted for them and looking much warmer.

Bob announced at that moment, that dinner was served, and what a dinner it was. Roast salt pork, followed by Christmas pudding, and then a slice of Christmas cake. Taken in two sittings, of course, as someone was on watch, all the time.

Finally, I asked the help of the lads of the second sitting to help Bob and me to solve the mystery of Captain Rhys Morris's present, which

Santa had apparently forgotten. Bob had helped me smuggle it aboard, – hiding something from the Captain of a ship is not easy!

When we came down from the watch, it was ready and waiting. A harmonium, for him to play, and now, we had a glass of Madeira wine apiece, and we sang, and sang, all the favourite songs and hymns, the Christmas carols, and we finished up with "Ar hyd y Nos".

My present from my beloved Rhys was this emerald ring, made of Welsh gold, which I have worn ever since, and for you, Rhian, the gold locket, which you must always wear, when you are grown, with the portrait of Tada and me, tucked inside. It was taken on our wedding day.

Finally, the officers, Brinley and Jacko, and Bob and the lads, had bought for me a diary, and so I have transferred my story to it. No ordinary diary, I can tell you. It is leather bound, and on the cover has NIA'S DIARY, with a glorious picture of a lady with flowing golden locks. I was so overcome; I hardly knew how to thank them, especially remembering the surprise New Year's gifts, which I still had hidden away for them. But more of that anon.

By this time, we had all forgotten the weather, but it was easier, and within two days, we were gliding towards the Islands in glorious sunshine.

And suddenly, there, in Nain's attic, I remembered that Christmas tree with its delightful momma kangaroo, and pwchie, as I soon christened her baby. I remembered, too, the cosy feel of my monkey suit.

I remembered crying bitterly when we got home, and Grandma De Winton, turning up her nose at the sight of my pyjama suit, stripped it from me, and, holding her nose, threw it into the boiler flames.

Just a foggy memory, but there, somewhere, in my mixed-up head.

I was puzzled, and intrigued, and I had completely forgotten the cleaning out I had meant to do.

December 31st 1905

Hogmanay. I don't know how Bob Roberts manages it, but he always has something tucked away for a celebration.

This time, it was haggis, – not quite a Scots one, as he confessed, but a Welsh variation.

He had opened a couple of tins of corned beef, added lots of chopped, browned onions, and some crushed ship's biscuits. Then he'd added some gravy and spices, hashed it all up, and stuffed it into a thin muslin bag which he'd made himself, and boiled it, before turning it out, stripped of the muslin. Rhys's second in command, the mate, nipping down from the deck, where he was on watch, had piped it in. His pipes weren't Scottish, either, they were Northumbrian pipes, but the effect was startling, just the same – and great fun. Brinley Hewitson, the Mate, is from north of Newcastle, but his mother comes from Nefyn.

Anyway, it set the tone for the evening, and we had a feast to remember.

The weather is perfect for scudding along, so we set all the sails, and for half an hour, either side of midnight, we were all on deck, but nobody officially on watch, just all on the 'qui vive'.

We were finishing our supper with cyflaith, which we all enjoyed tugging and smoothing into fantastic shapes, while it was still warm. I noticed the men making quite a few crocs and koalas for Rhian.

Finally I produced my presents for the men. Leather boots, and a leather pouch, for each of them, with a written plea not to repeat last voyage's tanning of sea-lions' skins when we reached the Chilean coast. They had the grace to look a little ashamed.

Our Northumbrian mate produced a "wee dram" of fine whiskey for all of us, to welcome the new year, and after that, the singing was so delightful, that a steam ship – a cruise ship I think – which passed by not too far away, was lined with passengers waving and applauding. It is surprising how seldom we sight other shipping so close. Still, I suppose we should not have spotted one another except for the Hogmanay entertainment on both ships.

On the stroke of midnight we all embraced, and ten minutes later your eyes, my Rhian, were tight shut, and we carried you down to your bed.

I read on, entranced. Tada and Mammy, Rhys and Nia: I was recalling that time when they had been my whole life. Uncle Bob, Brinley the Mate, and Jacko Beynon, next in line, together with the crewmen, Ifor, Davy, even Nain, they were all just bit-players, in those days.

January 15th 1906

It would be cold, and probably raining now, in mid-winter in Porthmadog. Here we are out in the middle of the Atlantic Ocean, heading south, and the sun shines most of the day.

The difficulty is to make sure that you are safe, my Rhian, Uncle Bob has made you a harness, so that you cannot slip overboard when playing on deck, in this lovely weather.

Fortunately, not being quite seven years old yet, you are not tall enough to climb into the rigging without someone to look after you – usually Davy, as he is the one who loves to climb, and turn somersaults and generally act like Mowgli, in the Jungle Book.

And as the sun goes down, I love to stand at the bows of the ship, with you beside me, looking forward to all the happiness that this life will bring.

I am thrilled, Rhian, to notice how eager you are to read. It's lovely for the two of us to be sitting together in the little seat that Bob Roberts has built for us, tucked in before the mainmast, for when the sun is shining. His little shelf that swings across your chair gives you something to put your writing things on, too.

When we reach Sydney I shall make sure to buy some adventure stories for you.

Watching you devour your stories makes me remember when I was a little girl. I was constantly quarrelling with Mother, because I wanted to change my library books every day.

That is one thing I don't think you and I will ever quarrel over, Rhian – unless we are both wanting to read the same book at the same time!

In truth, it doesn't seem at all that long since you were ploughing your way through Peter Rabbit, and now I am proud to see you busy with 'Alice in Wonderland', and 'Peter Pan'. I see too, that you have swapped your 'Jungle Book' for 'Stalky and Co.', and 'Treasure Island'. I think you'll find them harder going, but tremendously exciting.

I realised suddenly that yet again, this was a love that Mam and I could have shared. I had found Grandma De Winton just as scornful of 'fairy stories'!

February 11th 1906

Today is Rhys's birthday, so Bob has made a special tea. It is a long time since we were able to take on some fresh fruit and vegetables from the Cape Verde Islands, but Bob always has a treat stored away for these occasions. The cake he produced was made before we left home, judging by the amount of Courvoisier he had needed to keep it tasty.

The evening was rounded off in the best possible way as this day we are crossing the Line, and tea was followed by the boarding of 'Olwen' by Father Neptune and his wife. I must admit that Neptune had a distinctly Geordie accent which I recognised from its similarity to Brinley's dialect, while his wife had a beard just like Choccy Bob's.

Even you, Rhian, had crossed the Line before, but Neptune insisted that anyone who did so on his birthday anniversary merited a real welcome from the God of the Seas. They held Rhys down while they covered his face with a revolting shaving cream, made of grease and all sorts of rubbish, and then proceeded to shave him with a razor made from an old scallop shell.

It was all great fun, made the more enjoyable for the men by the fact that this was their Captain being manhandled, especially when the tin bath of water appeared, ready for the dousing of the victim.

Suddenly a little voice cut in "Leave my Tada alone", and you leapt up to attack Father Neptune and his Missus, and they fled from you, my brave Rhian, in fear and trembling.

February 23rd 1906

We did an informal test of your work, Rhian, thinking of the day next year when you will have to go to school. We don't want you to be left behind in your studies.

I was very pleased with your reading and writing, but I'm afraid we'll have to get down to some serious work on the sums: – my fault, probably. Words have always meant more to me than dry old figures.

After supper, before you go to bed each night, the lads have agreed to let you join them at cards, to get used to numbers, for a start.

February 28th 1906

Well, the eternal games of snap, pairs, and now whist are certainly claiming your attention, although I'm not sure whether the numbers or the boys themselves are the attraction.

I'm not sure either that you ought to be learning to call the Queen of Diamonds the Old Pisser!

I have a feeling that the lessons you will long remember are Ifor's naming of the planets and the stars in the beauty of the sky at night.

And the visit of Neptune, of course!

April 1st 1906

We have had a good following wind for some weeks now, and have been fairly buzzing along.

As we were all breakfasting this morning there was a shout from the watchman "Land Ho, Captain!" For a moment everyone shot to their feet, in excitement, and then Jacko cut in,

"April the first! Fools day!", the little devil! So we all sat down to our breakfast hash, again, laughing wryly.

"Captain!" came the cry again, and Rhys rose wearily from the table.

"Any other day I might have believed him, the scamp" he said, "We can't be far away".

Next thing it was all hands on deck, and we were sailing briskly towards the entrance to that magnificent harbour on which Sydney is built.

I hope you will remember, when you are grown up, Rhian, how beautiful the other side of the world can be.

I am sure you will, for we shall certainly sail here again, together, when you are older.

Sailing into Sydney Harbour is like sailing through the portals of heaven. The coves and beaches stretch for a thousand miles, from one headland to the other. The trees, the birds, all the animals, the flowers, are spectacular to watch, and while we are here, I shall try to make certain that we visit as many of the naturally beautiful areas as we can.

We dropped an anchor in Mosman's Bay, and when we had seen the doctors, and the Port authorities, and passed their inspections, we were eager to greet the small boats of the fruit peddlers. And what wonderful fruit: grapes, pineapples, mangos, as well as apples, pears, oranges and bananas.

We sailed down to the quays, near the Rocks, and there we found several other ships from Wales. We had already spotted "Angharad", captained by Glyn Parry, from Porthdinllaen, and his wife Helen, a friend of mine from College days; and the chaplain from the Mission to Seamen came along to welcome us, and to invite us to the Welsh Chapel, and there we found lots of friends, and made lots of new friends, too. On Sunday, all the time we were in Sydney, we went to chapel there, and sang our hearts out, and reminisced about home, or talked about the wonderful world that lay ahead for us to explore.

That first Sunday was especially exciting. We all ended up aboard "Angharad" for the christening of Glyn and Helen's new baby daughter. She was named Carys, and what a wonderful chorus of songs and hymns celebrated her christening.

By the next Sunday, many of our friends had sailed away, but we welcomed newcomers, and this time all congregated on "Olwen", and we had a delicious supper prepared by Bob, and yet again a noson lawen to raise the heavens.

Everyone admired the harmonium, and Rhys and I sang "Myfanwy", and lots of our favourite duets.

At the Chapel, who should we meet but my cousin Sandra, and Rhys's cousin Peter.

So many of our Porthmadog seamen have relatives here in Australia, and they are always eager for news of home. All the men are invited out for meals, and to see the city, so that in many ways it is just like home.

It brought back memories of our last trip to Australia, when you were a toddler, Rhian fach. Then, we landed first in Melbourne, and my cousin Trefor and his wife Jenny came down to the quay, and took us on a wonderful trip round the fruit stalls, and the meat and fish markets, before taking us to their home, where we were entertained by the whole family.

I enjoyed our visit so very much – but this time it's Sydney.

April 15th 1906

Today we visited Sandra's house. We went across the bay on the ferry, and that was really exciting. The trees here are of softer greens – more silvery – than at home in Wales. Sandra and her husband have a house perched up on a hill, and after lunch, we went for a walk through *the ravine, just behind. The Eucalyptus smell is quite overpowering, and even here in the city, we spotted possums in the bushes, and even one wallaby. Rhian was determined to find a kangaroo, complete with Pwchie, but we were out of luck. The noisy, brightly coloured birds are quite alarming sometimes. Sandra and her boys found us some egrets, cockatoos, kookaburras and even a pelican, down by the shore.*

Next week, the family will join us in the Botanical Gardens, and then the boys will have a chance to see the ship, and Bob has volunteered to make us a special tea.

April 22nd 1906

Today we visited the Botanical Gardens, and how delightful it was to wander round feeding the birds, and other animals. Rhian fed the little koala bears, in their cages, and the kangaroos, and wallabies, which were on display. I am always pleased to see strange creatures, but there is something in my heart which cries out for them to be free. Totally illogical!

Sandra and Eric, and the boys, love their life here in Sydney, and their enthusiasm certainly spread to Rhian. She clung to the young cousins like a limpet, and they proudly found her a kanga, with Pwchie!, and koala bears, bandicoots – all manner of God's creatures. Bob, as ever, did us proud, with Australian fruit salad, and Welsh pice ar y maen [welsh cakes cooked on a griddle] for tea followed by crempog – pancakes, which the young ones had great fun helping him to toss.

May 1st 1906

The ship is unloaded of her cargo now, and we are waiting to be assigned to a new dock, to load our new cargo. During these few days, Peter has come to take us to Coogee, where he and his wife Marian live. Rhys had managed to come with us, leaving Brinley Hewitson, and Jacko Beynon in charge. They will get their few days to visit friends when we get back to the ship. Peter's brother Malcolm had come to see us, too, and we had a fantastic break. We crossed on one of the ferries to the north shore of the harbour. They have a small boat, and so we were able to sail along the shore, where we saw seals, and duck-billed platypuses, and collected crayfish which Marian cooked for our tea.

Once again we marvelled at the beauty, and the strangeness, of this other side of the world, underlined when Peter spotted a shark, and brought us all in some haste out of the water. What excitement.

May 15th 1906

Olwen is fully laden once again, and on the tide, the day after tomorrow, we shall set off to round Cape Horn, bound for Valparaiso.

Last night, the shipmates had a last night out, here in Sydney, and tonight it is our turn.

Gwynn Jones, a friend from the Welsh Chapel is taking us to a valley near by, for a last memory of our visit.

May 16th 1906

What a night to remember!

We reached the hillside at the head of the ravine, just as dusk fell. The moon was coming up to its fullness, and as it rose in the velvet sky, we named the stars, showed Rhian the stars of the Southern Cross, when out of the trees below flew a bat-like creature. Rhian's hands shot up to cover her face, and then as she heard the flutter of wings, and felt Rhys's arms holding her safe, she quietly opened her eyes, and stared in wonder. Below us the flying foxes swarmed out of the woods, like people back home in Porthmadog crowding out of the Big Top, when the circus came on August Monday. On they came, too many to count, until the whole sky was black with them, and they flew off, and round and round in their search for food. At last they were gone, down the valley towards the sea, and Rhian's eyes were closing, so we drifted back down to the ship, and supper.

What a picture to take away with us.

Entranced, I read on, not quite able to decide whether I remembered baby Carys and her family, or whether it was so typical of Welsh seafaring life, that I was imagining that I remembered being there.

May 18th 1906

One day you will remember our reading lesson today with hoots of laughter, although at the time, my darling, you were most put out at being caught out by Tada when you read chasm as chasm, ch as in Charlie!

"Why don't they spell it properly, then." Was your rejoinder!

As we left Sydney we talked about Captain Cook, and of Magellan, Christopher Columbus, Amerigo Vespucci, Drake and Raleigh, and I'm sure many teachers would give their eye teeth to be able to show their pupils what you have seen.

One thing – I felt much closer to my beloved Mam, Nia, than I had done for a long, long time.

Up there in the attic, I sailed with them round the Horn – Cape Stiff, as Uncle Bob always called it.

They – no, we! – had had a very favourable run, and Nia described the islands past which we sailed till we arrived at the entrance to Valparaiso harbour.

June 27th 1906

The month is almost ended, and this evening we dropped anchor in Valparaiso.

With the sun setting over the sea, the beauty of the bay is enough to take your breath away, facing as it does to the north, rather than the west, as one would expect. It did not take long for some of our compatriots from Wales to spot us, sailing in, and we were greeted by Craig Robertson, of the Gipsy Queen, whose wife, Dilys, is a dear friend from my childhood days. Strictly speaking Gipsy Queen is no longer a Welsh ship, for she has been sold, and re-registered in Liverpool; Craig is a Scot, too, but I still feel they are part of our small world of Welsh sail.

They insisted that we must have supper with them that very evening, and I was delighted to see again their young son, who was born at sea some four years ago. What, I wonder, is the nationality of a small boy, son of a Scottish father born in Dundee, whose parents emigrated to Australia with him when he was just two years of age, and who became an Australian citizen, and whose Welsh wife gave birth to their little son in mid-ocean in a ship registered in Liverpool, England? First port of call after his birth, Tristan de Cunha. A ready born citizen of the world, to my way of thinking!

June 30th 1906

This is my first visit to Valparaiso. On the previous occasion when we rounded The Horn, Rhian, you were just a tiny girl, and we were loaded with coal for San Francisco, bypassing the Chilean and Peruvian ports.

Some day I shall tell you all about that trip, too, as we sailed into San Francisco, past the Golden Gate Bridge, and about our stop-over on the way home, in the Hawaiian Islands.

This is such a wonderful way of living: meeting people of every race, all over the world. And the world itself is so very beautiful.

Valparaiso is another magnificent bay, with rolling hillsides rising high above the water. The houses looking down to the sea show the Spanish influence and are quite grand, and the local people have acquired, too, the Spanish attitude, "Never do today what you could possibly put off until tomorrow"! Even Rhian knows the meaning of "mañana", after a mere two or three days here.

Poor Rhys is getting very anxious about the time it is taking us to get the cargo unloaded here.

I rather regret having mentioned that I think our next baby is conceived, and will arrive, I think, before the year's end!

It is just one more thing for Rhys to worry about: will we get home in time? This won't be the first baby born at sea, of course.

July 1st 1906

One of our first trips ashore was on Sunday when we rode in the funicular cars that run overhead, up the hillsides to the crest. We went with Craig and Dilys, to visit the grave of Craig's cousin. She had been lost four years before, when her husband's ship had been driven aground in a storm. She and her baby daughter had lost their lives, together with several of the crew. We noticed that there were flowers on all their graves. No doubt any sailor who knew of their deaths would think of them, so far from home.

That, of course is the down side of our lives at sea.

July 7th 1906

We were relieved to see Angharad *sail in on today's tide; we had expected her sooner.*

She had been slower to get away from New South Wales, having to go to Newcastle, further north, to load coal for Valparaiso, but as she had left Sydney before us, we were beginning to worry, when to our joy, she sailed in to port.

Now, we were delighted to greet Glyn Parry and Helen, and to dote on our beautiful Carys. She had come on tremendously since our days in Sydney, and now, at six months she is sitting up on her mother's lap, smiling and banging and clashing on the toy drum some well-wisher was unwise enough to give her.

All the passers-by are calling her "bonita niña", waving to her, and stopping to amuse her, as they delay getting down to work.

July 22nd 1906

For the last three weeks, while the ships were being cleared of their cargos, we ladies have enjoyed a real holiday.

We took a carriage, pulled by three horses, up English Hill, visited all the funicular lifts which ran us up to all the finest viewpoints.

On Sundays our whole families and friends met in Olwen's main cabin, and congregated round Rhys's harmonium, we sang hymns, and favourite songs, and told stories.

On the eve of Gipsy Queen's sailing for home, we were all invited aboard to a farewell party, and we enjoyed supper, and a real sing-song. Rhys and I sang our favourite "Myfanwy", Rhian sang "Y Fwyalchen [the blackbird]" – I hope you will recall your success when you read my diary, my darling.

We were all outshone by Gipsy Queen's mate, a young Scot, called Jamie Paterson, who sang a wonderful song by Robbie Burns,

"Oh wert thou in the cauld blast
On yonder lea, on yonder lea ... "

It was one neither Rhys nor I had heard before, and we insisted that the poor young chap must teach it to us. It will be our star performance, in future, along with "Myfanwy"!

It's not only we Welsh who can sing and write songs, – I'll tell you!

Next day we waved Gipsy Queen goodbye and safe journey, as she sailed for home.

July 27th 1906

Seven years old today. The time since you were born has passed so quickly, and with such delight, that Rhys and I can scarcely believe it, my darling.

You have blessed our love with such happiness, Rhian fach.

We spent today with all our friends from home. We swam in a little cove at the far side of the bay, had a picnic tea, and played games until it was time to go aboard again.

There we all sang songs at Tada's harmonium. It is such a pleasure to hear you, the young ones, singing our old songs, all over the world.

August 6th 1906

We have been on deck, with Rhian, encouraging her to wave her goodbyes to this lovely city. The sea is as still as a duck-pond. We are fully laden, just waiting for the formalities of the port authority's permission to leave, and a pilot to tow us out to deeper water. The weather has turned sultry and remarkably warm for winter time, though the sun is not breaking through the clouds. Rhys is getting anxious – there is so little wind, that we could spend all day beating our way, and getting nowhere.

I had to abandon my diary entry earlier, when we were suddenly surprised by a creaking and shuddering under our feet. There was no breeze worth speaking of, no run of the currents in the seas about us.

Bob laughed "Must be a whale, scratching his back on our barnacled bottom!"

Suddenly Olwen began to tremble and rattle: it was as if the poor old girl's teeth were chattering, according to Jacko.

As we stood there on the deck, Rhys grasped me tight in his arms, Rhian close between us, as the growling noise broke out again.

"Down, Rover!" joking from Ifor, this time, who was at the helm, awaiting the pilot.

As we all watched, the whole shore line exploded into the sky! Little spurts of fire were sparking all over the city. Smoke clouds, constant rumble-grumble, followed suddenly by a moment of deadly silence, broken almost at once by the cries of people in mortal distress, dogs barking in terror, horses whinnying. The growling had lasted only about five minutes, but it seemed a lifetime.

And then the quaking began again, and over and over, right through the night. All the time the heart-breaking screams of children and mothers, of animals, drowned out gradually by the crash of buildings, people's homes, just crumbling to nothing, burying many of the families below.

The Mole, which stretched out into the harbour leapt into life, with whole families rowing out into the bay, to get away from the land. We have taken aboard all those who managed to reach us, but many more are just getting as far out to sea as they can.

The noise from the city is undiminished. The homes round the shore are just heaps of rubble, on fire, and the tall houses on the hillsides are starting to turn to dust. The roar of the flames is everywhere, as they shoot up into the dark clouded sky.

August 7th 1906

It is morning, though no-one would know, for the heavens are as black as ever, but at least the quaking has stopped. Rhys is in charge, here on board, and Bob and I are cooking broth, and finding what we can spare of our stores, to feed the families who have managed to reach us. Brinley, Jacko and Ifor have each taken a boat with a couple of the crew ashore, to see what we can do to help. All is quiet at last, and once we have fed them, our visitors are struggling back to see what is left of their homes.

More trouble ahead. We have just been warned by the harbour master that there will be tidal waves from the sea, to follow the earthquake! As a precaution the engineer who runs the power station has switched off the electricity: rightly, too. The last thing these people need is electrical trouble. The fires are still raging, and buildings and food stores are gone, and considering the desperation of their plight, there has been no looting or pillaging.

We have just noticed that the steamers are all motoring away, out to sea to dodge the great waves that are forecast. It is a tempting thought, but the wind and tides are not right for us. Instead, we are offering to take those who are still aboard, and have no homes to go to, and land them somewhere more favourable, when we can finally get away, but they are all wanting to stay here, to go to look for their friends, and to rebuild their lives. The thought of a land on the other side of the world is frightening, of course: "Better the Devil we know ... ".

We have supplied our visitors with almost all the fresh water in our tanks, and all the food we can spare, each man of our crew offering to eat and drink less, until we can get stores.

The first of the tidal waves had rolled in. Olwen *was thrown high on the cresting wave, and then the seas avalanched over the deck. Fortunately, we were all below in time, and Rhys had insisted that everyone of us was lashed to something, but with the means of getting free, should the ship show signs of succumbing to the onslaught of the waters.*

Fortunately, too, the anchor held, right through the succession of great rollers that pounded us in the next few hours.

Rhian, perhaps you remember, my darling, counting, "uno, due ... ", and then reverting to your Welsh when we got to ten; I think we counted eighteen in all, the last few, thankfully growing less violent.

There was no way we could just sail off and leave these good people to face things alone, so all hands reported on shore, and set to rescue those we could. A crew of strong young men were a help to shift some of the heavy boulders and timber; I hope some of the tragic sights they faced will not haunt them, later on.

Rhys has decided that we must get away on the next tide. There is danger from cholera and other diseases which usually follow such disasters, and it will not help anyone for us to sail out and spread the illnesses throughout the world.

August 8th 1906

We got away on the morning tide, after a real struggle to lift the anchor.

I hope Angharad *and* Gipsy Queen *were out of the reach of the disaster, thinking particularly of the children aboard. Just in case, we set extra men on deck for the next few days, keeping watch for lifeboats, or rafts. Rhian is entranced with this procedure – she thinks it's much more fun than sums or reading lessons, with me.*

August 9th 1906

The troubles of our visit to this coast seem to be behind us at last. We are heading south, for Tierra del Fuego, past the myriad islands of this coast of Chile, backed behind by the Andean peaks, reaching up high into the sky.

"I can't help wondering what happened to those cousins of our, Rhys", I said. "The ones who went to live in Patagonia, yn Y Wladfa, all those years ago. I wonder whether the children and grandchildren speak Welsh or Spanish?"

August 10th 1906

What a day this has been.

We were heading south, and you were beside me, Rhian, at the bow of the ship, watching the sun come up. I had drifted off into a dream, when I felt you tugging my dress.

"Mam, Mam, there's something there – can you see?" "There's something in it, too. Is it the Old Man of the Sea?"

I stared and stared, then called for Rhys and the men. Below us, tossing on the waves was a raft, with a body aboard.

Then, suddenly, as if the noise of our excitement had called him back, his eyelids fluttered, a hand moved.

I have no time to write more tonight.

August 11th 1906

I called out, "Rhys, Rhys, come quickly", and long before I had finished, the ship's boat was overboard, and even you, Rhian, were forgotten for a short time, while we hoisted the creature aboard.

Just as we were deciding we were too late, came a shrill little voice "Hobgoblin, hobgoblin, wake up! You are with Mam and Tada and me, now." Your voice dragged him back from the gates of Hell, his eyelids flickered again, and then sunken blue eyes were gazing at us in bewilderment.

His lips moved painfully, but no sound came out.

We started him off on water, dropped into his mouth with a spoon, then gradually with a little honey and sugar added.

You, Rhian, would not leave his side, and he held on to your hand and mine, as if to convince himself that we were real.

The raft was just three pieces of old, battered driftwood, bound together with seaweed, and the same straggling weeds had secured him to the raft, and covered his body from the scorching sun – somewhat inadequately. His whole body was a mass of boils and scars, raw patches of flesh, some of them festering really badly, and his hair had been drawn forward to protect his face from the scorching sun, and the salt sea water.

There was nothing at all on the raft to tell us who he is. He obviously is not one of the wretched Chinese slaves, who work the guano deposits on the Chincha Islands, nor does he seem to be of Indian origin; in fact he seems to be European, but we could not be certain.

Given the devastation left by the earthquake, Valparaiso was no place to take him ashore, so we went on our way, intending to round the Horn, and then perhaps call in at Buenos Aires, or Rio. In the meantime, he has slept for twenty four hours, and then, anxious that he might slip away, Bob and I woke him, and gave him fluids and sugar, once more.

Rhian, who had abandoned him only when carried off to bed, surreptitiously gave him a mouthful of her chewed up toffee, since this was the last she had left, and luckily this seems to have been the right moment.

Shortly afterwards he was able to tackle a dish of porridge, with a little condensed milk. Before drifting off to sleep again, he told us that he is a Finn, sailing on his father's ship.

August 13th 1906

By the time our shipwrecked mariner awoke again, Rhian had been persuaded that he might be sad at being called 'Hobgoblin'; she had christened him 'Finn', instead.

It is a little unnerving: he looks at me as if I were a vision from another world, and our lads have decided that he is a good luck man: since we picked him up, we have had following winds, and are racing for home in great style. He woke up, quite panic-stricken. He remembered being found by us, but little else of his nightmare.

He spoke only broken English, but was at last able to tell us that he comes from the Åland Islands, lying at the very North of the Baltic Sea, between Finland and Sweden. His father was master, and owner of his ship, "Sigyn", and his two younger brothers were with them, on this voyage, for their first trip.

At this point, his face twisted with misery, as he recalled, and told us what had happened to them.

They had had to travel up to Callao, on the coast of Peru to get a cargo for home. It was to be guano – every seaman's nightmare cargo, and they had queued, along with a long line of small ships of all the nations of the world, for weeks, before their turn came to load.

Even then, it had taken weeks for the poor Chinese workers to shuttle the smelly bird-muck to fill the holds. Finally, they had had to return to Callao for orders, before sailing for home.

While there, his crew had insisted on going for a last night ashore. In their cups, they had been taken by the crimps. Worried for the safety of his three sons, Captain Carlsen, had decided to sail off, and try to ship a new crew at the nearest safe port. The crimps, angry at not being able to sell him a new crew, must have followed them, and ten days later, they had attacked Sigyn, boarded her, killed his father, set fire to his twin brothers, and keelhauled Finn himself, having stripped him of his clothes. Then believing him dead, they had thrown him back into the ocean, and sailed off in Sigyn.

Finn had been near enough to the landmass to find the few planks of driftwood, and the seaweed, and had drifted for goodness know how many days and nights, before Rhian sighted his raft. He had survived on rain water, and one bird, which had landed on his raft on the second day. He had felt the tidal waves which followed the earthquake, but must have been far enough away, not to feel the quake itself.

September 3rd 1906

Finn, whose name is really Mika Carlsen, we now know, is improving day by day. When I look at him, joining in as a crew member, it is difficult to realise how near to death he was when we found him.

He is a fine seaman – a great help to our crew – and accepted by them already, as a lifetime friend.

The name Finn has stuck with him, to humour Rhian.

He has joined Ifor and Davy on their watch, being 16 years old, just a shade older than Ifor.

We have abandoned the idea of calling in at Buenos Aires when the time comes, at Finn's suggestion. He feels that if his mother has heard of *the loss of* Sigyn, *she will not want to wait all the weeks that must pass before he can get home to her. If she still expects them all home, then he believes that he cannot risk telling her of the tragic happenings, that it will be easier for her if he is there, and I must say that I feel he is right.*

It will take great courage, though.

She has one young son still at home, and a new baby which was expected just after they had sailed, so she is not entirely alone.

September 15th 1906

We have rounded Cape Horn, and are racing for home. Yesterday we passed two ships from Caernarfon, Bethan, *and* Alwyn. *We are certainly favoured with every breath of wind taking us home, on this trip.*

I suddenly realised that the sun was coming up, gleaming golden through Nain's green flowered curtains.

I had been roused from my travels in *Olwen* by the clip-clop of Maggie Ty-Canol's horse pulling the milk cart, and stopping at the street door, to fill the milk jug.

I looked around – well, there's always another day for tidying up, as Nain says, but no guarantee that you'll find anything as interesting to read again. So I buried my head once more in Mam's diary.

The voices of children on their way to school were in my ears, as we came to the end of the voyage.

The word jumped to my eyes.

December 3rd 1906

We sailed into Cardiff docks the night before last, and as soon as humanly possible, Rhys brought me here, to the Glossop Terrace maternity hospital. I am in bed in the ward, and our new baby is due at any moment.

When the baby is born, Mother will come down to stay with cousins in Colum Road, and as soon as Baby is well enough to travel, we shall take the train up to Porthmadog.

Rhian is still on board ship, but she will come to Cousin Gwenda's house in Colum Road, when I get out of hospital.

My diary of the voyage is finished here, and I think I shall ask Rhys to tuck it away in my seaman's box, until we get home to Chapel Street, when you, Rhian fach, can keep it, and read it in the years to come.

That was Mam's diary finished.

I knew only too well what happened that night. Mam was taken into theatre, because of complications in the delivery of the baby.

The only time I saw her again, she was a waxen statue of herself, lying in her coffin.

I promised her that I would look after our baby boy, then I climbed up on a chair, and kissed my lovely Mam, a last kiss.

Tada, Grandma De Winton, and I travelled up with the coffin, and Mam was buried in the cemetery in Moel-y-Gest.

Tada had to go back to the ship, and Grandma De Winton brought Owen and me straight to Maeshyfryd, where a nurse looked after Owen, until he was a year old.

Now, in a fit of anguish, I set to and scoured the attic from roof to floor, careful, though to put Mam's box with all its precious contents safely away.

Below, I heard the door open, the milk collected and put into the pantry, and then,

"Rhian annwyl, are you there? Are you all right?"

I went downstairs to find breakfast on the table ready for me.

"I found Mam's diary," I said, "in her sea-box," and it was obvious at once that Nain had not know of the diary.

Chapter Twenty-one

The morning passed like a flash, while I told Nain about Mam's diary.

"It explains so much about Finn", I said. "But why did he come back to Porthmadog with Tada? Was it because Nia died? Didn't he want to stay to help his Mam?"

Nain looked at me sadly. "No, cariad," she sighed. "The terrible things that happened to that young boy shook even my belief in a God that is good."

I looked at her in consternation.

"Come and sit with me on the couch here," she said, and she held me close, my head on her heart.

"How that young man has grown into the loving, caring man that he is now, is what restored my faith."

"You know, now, how Finn came to be with you all aboard *Olwen*. When Nia died, and you and her baby, Owen, went to live with your Grandma in Maeshyfryd, Rhys, your father, left Brinley and Jacko to see to the re-loading, and he went straight away to the island at Åland, taking Finn home to his mother. They arrived there, but found themselves waylaid by Finn's grandfather. It seemed that those wicked crimps had claimed that they had found *Sigyn* adrift, had boarded her, only to discover the entire crew dead from yellow fever."

I gasped in horror. "Surely no one would believe them! Not without checking up."

"They were believed, because their description of the Master and his sons, and the crew, were accurate. Everyone thought they could not have made it up. They said, because of the fever, and the risk of passing it on, they had to bury them all at sea, they claimed *Sigyn* as salvage."

I was a jump ahead of Nain, and found myself still wondering "Didn't Finn want to stay, and help his Mam?", I asked.

"In a way, that was the saddest thing of all", said Nain, "His mother, poor lady, had been so devastated by the news of the death of all her loved ones, that she went a little bit doolallie."

Nain, making excuses for everyone, I smiled quietly to myself.

"She was grieving so much over the death of her husband, and she had one young boy there, and the new baby she was expecting turned out to be twin boys: somehow she blotted out the memory of the three boys who had sailed with their father. She insisted that these three tinies were Mika, Eric and Carli."

"She wasn't a mother! She was an old witch!" I burst out.

"No, no, cariad", Nain stopped me. "I can understand. Her whole world had disappeared with that ship, and yet she had to carry on, with no money, no insurance because of the salvage claim, a wee boy who only reminded her of what she had lost, and then two new little ones to feed and clothe, and keep a roof over their heads. I'm sure she put them out of her world, because, loving them so, she couldn't carry on any other way."

"When she caught a glimpse of Finn, as he went one night, hoping to see his home, without disturbing his poor mother, she rushed out with a cross, and a burning candle, to exorcise the evil ghost come to torment her. She had been driven out of her mind with fear and sorrow, and thought he had come to steal her three little boys."

Nain looked up at me. "So there he was. Alone."

Chapter Twenty-two

At first I had found myself getting more and more angry at how evil people could destroy a young man's life, but as I heard the whole story my heart seemed to slide into a great pit of sadness. Not only for Finn, and for his little brothers, and for his father, who had had to watch them burned to death, unable to help them, but for his poor mother, too. Which of us could live with those memories? But she had to: she had three little boys to care for.

Nain was visiting one of her friends that afternoon and in a fit of misery I marched off round the Cei, and over the sands as far as Morfa Bychan – not wandering along as I usually do, admiring the flowers, the birds, and the rolling waves, but stomping away, as if I could destroy the unhappiness in our world. Indeed, it did seem that everything was changing, and not for the better. No more sailing ships were built in Porthmadog. *Gestiana*, the last ship from any of the yards had been launched just after *Nia Ben Aur*, and now the iron or steel vessels had taken over, and the quays below me lay still and lifeless. The last loads of slate stood end to end, on the dock, and for the moment the trên bach still puffed its way over the embankment. Each springtime, the jumbled rocks of Ballast Island flowered anew. Some saw the exotic blossoms as a sad reminder of a wonderful age gone forever, but Nain always said "What dies away will spring into life again, but only when the time is right". In fact, one of the songs that Rhiannon and I had concocted all those months – no years – ago, was a setting of Robert Herrick's.

"Fair daffodils, we weep to see
You haste away so soon ... " We sang it for Nain, because it was one of her favourite poems, I remembered.

I got home just in time for supper, and found Finn sitting there telling Owen and Griff the story of his trip to South Georgia. I stood, unseen, in the doorway listening. Griff was sitting on the brass stool near the fender, and the fire was glowing with warmth. Tada's chair was empty, and Owen was propped up sitting on the floor, leaning against it. Nain's comfy padded chair held her knitting, and her open book, and judging from the smells from the kitchen, she was making a bit of supper. Finn was on the couch, where I usually sat to read.

"When I'm grown up, and I go sailing, I'll bring Nain a lovely soft fur coat to keep her warm in the winter ... " Owen was pontificating.

Finn grimaced "Oh, I don't think Nain Sarah likes fur" he said.

I cut in "No think of all those little foxes or bunny rabbits dead. I should buy her a silk dress"

"Oh, never mind all those little silkworms, wriggling homeless, 'cos their webs have disappeared ... " Owen laughed back at me.

I got a lovely smile from Finn, too, and then I realised that Nain was preparing a real Scouts' supper, and in two rat-tats at the door the house was full up with Owen's friends, busy eating faggots and pickled onions, followed by cacen pwdin [*bread pudding*], which I helped Nain to dish up.

Once my usefulness in the kitchen was done, "Sit down and keep quiet", I was instructed by my imperious little brother, and Finn started telling them more about his Antarctic trip.

Chapter Twenty-three

I thought what a wonderful big brother he must have been to those twin boys – how close they would have been as they sailed off, full of excitement, on that first voyage with their Father and brother Mika. And now he was telling these boys about Shackleton and his men struggling across the fury of the icy Antarctic Ocean, to find help on South Georgia.

The questions came thick and fast.

"How big is South Georgia, – as big as Wales?"

"How far from Elephant Island?"

A moment of quick calculation from Finn, then, "South Georgia is about a hundred miles from one end to the other. Wales is half as long again, roughly. Elephant Island is about 800 miles from South Georgia and it took Captain Shackleton and his five companions more than two weeks, in their little boat before they sighted the coast of South Georgia. Even then, they were on the wrong side of the island, but the boat was done for, so they had to land in King Haakon's Bay, and climb over the mountains and the glaciers, to the whaling station."

"Are the mountains higher than Snowdon?"

"Some of the mountains in South Georgia are twice as high as Snowdon, but the pass they had to climb over was only about as high as Rhyd-ddu, but it was covered in snow and ice, and no-one had drawn maps to show where they were going. Three of the men stayed with the boat, but Captain Shackleton and the two strongest men set out again, to find help. It took them a day and a half, to get to the other side, to Stromness, and then the first two young boys to spot them thought they were ghosts, and ran away."

"Did they rescue the three men left at the boat?"

"Yes, though the fellows didn't recognize Frank Worsley when he landed to rescue them – he was too clean and tidy."

"I couldn't help cutting in, "Didn't we meet Frank Worsley, when we were in Plymouth, with Tada, when Captain Shackleton said you could take *Nia Ben Aur* over to Newfoundland?"

"Yes, you met several of the men. Do you remember – Frank Wild, as well, and Uncle Bob's friend, Alfie, from Liverpool, and Chippy, the one with the cat?"

Owen's face lit up. "Yes, now I remember. Were they all rescued?" he asked, suddenly afraid.

"Every single one was rescued in the end," Finn reassured him.

"We went first in the *Southern Sky*, from Stromness, from the whaling station, but we ran out of fuel before we could get there, so Captain Shackleton went straight to Port Stanley, to look for a more suitable ship. We had four tries, before the *Yelcho* managed to get through, and we found everybody still alive, on Elephant Island."

"Were you there when they were rescued, Finn?" asked Griff. "I thought it was a ship from Chile."

"So it was," Finn replied, "but I was one of the seamen who tried, with the *Emma*, because we thought a schooner built in the old-style, in oak, might prove better. The Chilean Government lent Captain Shackleton the *Yelcho*, to tow us part of the way, but we couldn't get through, and so we had to return to Punta Arenas. Shack felt it was going to be too late, by the time the *Discovery* sailed from Britain, so we made one last try, with the *Yelcho*. It didn't seem right for men with families to support to risk everything, so one or two of us took the place of the usual crew.

It was wonderful to get to Elephant Island, and find them there on the beach, in the snow and the fog which had nearly made us miss the camp altogether. Then to find we were in time to save them all, to get every one of the crew and expedition members aboard, and safe.

One of the crew I hadn't met before was a Welshman, who'd stowed away when they left Buenos Aires: They'd cut off his toes, because of frost-bite, but he was soon walking about again, when we got back to Punta Arenas.

What a welcome we had from the people of Chile, when we got back. They let Captain Shackleton borrow the *Yelcho*, to go up to Valparaiso, and that's where I left them to come home."

"What do people do on a whaling station?", asked Griff.

"Catch whales, dumbo!", came from Robyn Meredith.

"No, I mean it's a long way away to be going to catch whalemeat …", explained Griff.

"Nowadays," said Finn, "whales and seals too, are caught as much for their blubber, as for the meat. The blubber makes soap, and margarine … "

"We have butter from Maggie Tŷ-Canol, and I'd just as well do without soap, thank you very much … " muttered Owen.

"I gather it's used to make nitro-glycerine, for explosives, to help with the war effort," Finn glance over mischievously at me, "and of course the whalebone is needed for corsets. What would the ladies do without their stays!"

I pretended to threaten him with my easel and paint brushes, which I was just taking up to the attic, raising howls of laughter from the boys.

By the time I came down again the boys had gone home and Owen was trying to persuade Nain to let him stay up the remaining hour till midnight with his friend Finn, but Nain shooed him off, and Finn went up to see his room.

For once, I couldn't wait to see them go. I showed Nain what I had found in Mam's box. Her jewel case, with her wedding ring, and my gold locket, with the picture of Nia and Tada, newly married, and of Nain and me. I had brought the diary, too, for her to read.

Finn came down at this point, having measured up the space in Owen's room, to get timber from David Williams' yard, to build bookshelves for Owen next day.

Chapter Twenty-four

Jenny and I had promised to call at our old school next day, and I went off at the same time as Owen. Nain came down just in time to see us leave. She was enjoying having me at home, I knew, for it meant she could have a little lie-in, while I got Owen his breakfast.

This morning she had the look of one who has hardly slept, and as she was hugging Mam's diary, I knew why. I gave her a special smile, and a caress, as I said goodbye.

Peredur was with Jenny. His ship had docked in Cardiff a day or two earlier, and he had dashed up to Porthmadog as soon as he could get away.

Owen started running as soon as we caught sight of him, and flung his arms around Peredur. I started to race to do the same, when I saw the bemused look that Jenny threw me, and I hesitated.

"Oh, go on, Rhian," she grinned, so I too was enveloped in Peredur's arms. I had the grace to look a little apologetic, as we drew apart, but she laughed at us.

"If you really think I'm going to get shipwrecked with Peredur to get even with you two, you're elevenpence short of the shilling!" she teased, and we all four walked to school hand in hand, spread across the lane, so that Hugh Pôst's geese had to wait to get past us.

We had a memorable morning at school, and Peredur and Jenny came back to have some dinner with us. Nain can always find something to entertain friends, even in the middle of a war. Jenny must have been amused to find Peredur given the same warm welcome once again, this time by Finn, who was upstairs fixing Owen's shelves when we got there.

I said nothing about Nia's diary, because I hadn't had a chance to tell Owen yet, nor Finn, who was so much involved, so the afternoon passed in chatter bringing everyone up to date. Ifor had got his Master's ticket, and was in command of his first ship – just coasting, while the war continued. Uncle Bob had agreed to join him, just until the war was won when he would retire. No-one dared ask what would happen if we lost!

Rhiannon was with the Opera, in London. Jenny had heard that her poet-friend had been called into the army, and had met her in London, on his way over to France, to the trenches.

We were all sitting in the kitchen over the cleared table, by this time, Finn having finished the bookshelves, Owen having reluctantly disappeared back to school. As soon as Jenny and Peredur left, Nain lifted the diary on to the table.

"I think Finn might read Nia's diary, next, she suggested, and then between you two, you must help Owen to understand. Suddenly, she put her head on her arms on the table, and the tears crept down her cheeks.

"I am sorry, my darling" she whispered, as I took her into my arms.

"So stupid to have outlived them both, my Rhys and his lovely Nia. Owen and you, my sweetheart, you have no-one to watch out for you except me – and I'm so old."

The tears burst from her again, and then I was clasped in her arms.

"A beth amdanaf fi?" "What about me?" a strong voice, deep and warm, like brown velvet cut in. Strong arms were around Nain, and she smiled falteringly.

"Oh, if there is any light at all in this darkness in my heart, it's from you two and Owen it comes", and she smiled tremulously.

I lifted my head from Nain's lap, and there stood Finn. He was smiling tenderly at Nain, and suddenly I knew I loved him. I shut my eyes, for fear of giving myself away, and looked for my hankie … couldn't find it. Never can, when I need it! I wiped my nose surreptitiously with the back of my hand, and looking up, shamefaced, I caught Finn looking at me – a look of laughter at my predicament. He tried to look away as I smiled sheepishly, but it was as if he was held by magnets. What I saw in his eyes … I dared not believe … understanding … hope … joy … love? My hand somehow crept into his hand. I couldn't make myself turn away from him.

Nain looked at us. She saw what we were too shy to say, and she swept us both into her arms.

We were all three laughing, smiling, crying all at once. I kissed Nain, and then almost unable to stop myself, I reached up, and kissed Finn shyly, on his cheek.

Before I could turn away, he pulled Nain and me closer, and kissed me, and suddenly that strange reserve that had always been part of his kindness to me was shattered. He kissed me full on the mouth, again and again – for I was kissing him back. He was whispering endearments to me, his hands caressed my face.

Suddenly, I was back on the seas, looking at the raft. But it wasn't our raft ... there was a boy on it ... and as I looked, his eyes fluttered, and Mam was standing beside me as I shouted, "Mam, mam, there's a boy in the water ... "

My face must have shown what I was remembering. I said "On the raft ... the boy ... Mam running for the boat ... sitting with your head on her heart",

"Making mine beat ... making me live." Finn cut in.

"It wasn't because of you that I forgot," I said. "It was just that I couldn't get on with the life I had left, when I remembered how much she loved me, and I loved her. If I hadn't promised her that I would look after Owen, I don't think I could have gone on ... I think I might have given up, and followed her to Tir na'n Og."

"But she made me promise to care for him, and a promise is a promise ... especially one made to her."

Finn held me closer than ever, in his arms. He held my face up, and looked deep into my eyes.

"I made no promises", he said. "I love you. I shall always love you, whatever you may choose to do."

Chapter Twenty-five

We couldn't be together, of course, not straight away. But from the day we admitted our love for one another my life became a fairy tale of happiness.

When Finn had to go back to sea, for there was still a war to be finished, I worried about his safety, but somewhere in my mind was a certainty that we were meant to be together.

Jenny and I passed our exams, and started teaching – Jenny in Wrexham, and me – where else but Bootle!

The armistice came, but just before it the most heartbreaking of events.

The Eisteddfod was being held in Birkenhead.

The subject for the cywydd (an ancient form of Welsh poetry) was 'Yr Arwr' (the hero) and when the archdruid called the ffug-enw (*nom de plume*) of the victor, he cried "Safed ar ei draed" (let him stand up), but no-one stood up.

"Safed ar ei draed", again, and once more, no-one. The third command, and then it was announced that the bard to be chaired was Hedd Wynn, Rhiannon's friend, from Trawsfynydd. He had been called up, into the army, and was fighting in France.

Just days later, the war was over.

Hedd Wynn had died in the trenches just hours before his Chair was won.

It was July, in the year after the end of the war, before Finn could leave his ship, and we could plan to get married. I had wanted as many as possible of our friends to be able to come, so we sent out lots of invitations in plenty of time.

We planned things so that Ifor and Peredur would be able to join us, and Guto too. Uncle Bob gave me away, standing in for Tada, as he had done in those weeks on the raft, he and Finn of course. Finn had his best man in attendance, too: a proud as a peacock Owen, now approaching thirteen years of age.

The clan MacLeod came in force, and they travelled across from Newfoundland with Marrion and the Twinks. Tada's two little girls were as different from one another now as they had been when we first saw them, in Rainbow Tickle, except that they had swapped over. Sarah was now the taller of the two, and definitely the boss! They had bridesmaid's dresses, as pretty as any picture, made for them by Nain, and they carried tiny baskets of flowers. When we were still celebrating, at five o'clock in the morning after the wedding, their two little faces were visible; sitting on the stairs in their nighties, they were watching intently – laughing and joining in the fun. Only Cathy had not been able to come. Perhaps she hadn't wanted to come to Porthmadog ever again. Marrion told me she had heard not a word from Llew Bulkeley during the remainder of the war. Mr. Parry, the lawyer who had found us Nia's sea chest had taken on the management of Tada's estate, with William Lloyd's help, and had looked after us, and Tada's loved ones in Rainbow Tickle.

We had been able to invite "Grandma" Rosa Elkan, too, and a few of our friends from Hamburg. Some people were very much against renewing the old friendships, especially as there were no longer sailing ships taking slates across the North Sea from Porthmadog, but we reminded them how the Elkan family, and others like them, too, had risked their lives to help the Welsh ships out of port, on that first night of war. The danger they had saved us from was only too clear – the ships and their crews that had not got away had never been heard of again.

Jenny was my bridesmaid. I had asked Rhiannon to join her, but she was due to perform the next week, and sent her apologies.

"I'll definitely come," she wrote, "but don't hang about waiting for me, I'll be late."

I walked down the aisle in Anita's dress, the one she gave me when we reached Carbonear. It had always retained a magic for me, and her face lit up when she saw it. I wore my engagement ring – that wonderful emerald, set in Welsh gold, and my locket, with its pictures, and our wedding ring, when Finn slid it on my finger, was Mam's wedding ring.

I should have known of course. Uncle Bob helped me down from the pony and trap – the same one that Finn had brought to the station to welcome us home before. I took Bob's arm, and as I started down the aisle, the little organ fell silent, and Rhiannon's voice soared into heaven, filling the Chapel with music to beguile the soul of the most demanding of gods. I stood for a moment in sheer delight, and then paced eagerly forward to my awaiting love.

Later that week, we went south to Cardiff. After our years of loneliness, we were determined that our children would grow up with their father coming home every night, and sharing their lives. Peredur, with the same thoughts in mind, had decided to join the lighthouse service, and he and Jenny had been offered the South Stack light, once he had completed his training. When we visited them, I was not surprised to find airplane models everywhere, and a helicopter model, too.

Finn had accepted a post with a firm importing timber, in Cardiff, and we would live at first, in the front room of Davy's auntie's house, while we waited to be allowed to rent a council house. Jenny and I were not permitted to teach, of course once we married, as there were so many men coming back from the war, who would want work, to bring up their families.

To be together was what mattered to Finn and me.

An End and a Beginning

It was night time, and the skies were dark, as Finn called "I'm home cariad. No pains yet?"

"Not desperate, any way" Rhian answered.

"The girls are doing their homework." She added, "Finn, my love, do you realise, just two more weeks, and this baby will share your birthday, on the first day of February!"

"Not the year, though, eh, Mam. This is 1941!", came a voice from the sitting room, where the girls were doing their homework.

By the time midnight came, the girls were shaking the sleep out of their eyes. Moaning Minnie, the siren, had wearily warned of trouble, yet again. The little fire bombs hissed and banged, exploding all round the crossroads.

In the street, Finn Carlsen, one of the few able-bodied men left to help fight the fires, since all the younger ones were called up, dashed to the nearest fire with his stirrup-pump and bucket. A chain was made up in no time at all, his three teen-age daughters among the youngsters passing the pails of water hand to hand from the nearest tap to the stirrup pump.

In the kitchen at number ten Rhian prepared some warm soup, and a flask of tea for when they came home. They would be cold and weary.

Rhian tied on her blue and white pinny, which would barely meet round her middle now. She hoped the baby would come soon, and more than anything else, she hoped it would be a boy, at last. Without the child, she could have gone back to teaching, like Jenny, filling the places left by the men who had been called to fight this war, but she still felt that a child came before all else.

Until these last few weeks, she would have been with them, outside, but with the birth so close, she had been persuaded to stay inside.

"What if you started your pains, out there in the street. We'd have to drop the fire fighting and get you home" Finn had remonstrated with her. So now, she had to stay indoors, and she compromised by putting things ready in the kitchen, while keeping the door to the 'cwch dan stâr [*hiding place under the stairs*]' open for emergencies.

At first she had suffered nightmares thinking they would be killed, all her loved ones, and never come back, but you get used to any situation, given time, she marvelled to herself.

In the skies above, a German plane – a late one, left behind the main squadron, droned overhead.

Who knows – perhaps he saw the fires which were just about doused, perhaps it was just an idle whim, – he decided to loose the bombs … now!

They whistled down, landed with a great boom of menace, and a volcano of flame burst into the dark.

Finn and his girls raced home. Nothing left but a great hole in the ground, and the mangled remains of a home-made blue and white pinny, halfway into the 'cwch dan stâr'.

Then, a faint whimper, the wee baby had outlived his Mammy.